Lock Down Publications and Ca$h
Presents

I0666807

BAD B*TCHES WIT' GUNZ

LICENSED TO KILL

Written By
Christopher "Diesel" Hornezes

CHRISTOPHER "DIESEL" HORNEZES

First Edition 2025

Printed in the United States of America

Lock Down Publications
P.O. Box 944
Stockbridge, GA 30281
www.lockdownpublications.com

Like our page on Facebook: Lock Down Publications
www.facebook.com/lockdownpublications.ldp

Stay Connected with Us!

Text **LOCKDOWN** to 22828 to stay up-to-date with new releases, sneak peaks, contests and more...

Like our page on Facebook:
Lock Down Publications

Join Lock Down Publications/The New Era Reading Group

Visit our website:
www.lockdownpublications.com

Follow us on Instagram:
Lock Down Publications

Email Us: We want to hear from you!

Chapter 1

"Oh, shit! Aye, is that Twelve behind us?" asked Hot Boy, panicking after witnessing the black Lincoln Navigator slip in behind his Jeep Trackhawk.

Riding shotgun next to him in the passenger's seat, Mario looked in his mirror and saw it. He chuckled to himself, shaking his head. "It might be," Mario replied, nonchalantly, looking in his mirror, though not worried about it. "Just be cool, drive right and we'll be okay, my nigga."

Travelling through Chicago on the Dan Ryan Expressway, the two young Colombian drug traffickers were riding super dirty in a Hellcat-engine-equipped SUV. Throughout the Jeep, there were a hundred bricks of pure Colombian cocaine, packed into various trap-spots around the interior. The two were en route to make a drop-off to one of their boss's clients. They both had Glock .40s, fitted with extended 30-round clips, filled with hollow points, locked and ready to pop anyone that tried them.

Hot Boy, though, was nervous. He hated cops. He didn't want to go back to prison. Mario hated how Hot Boy lacked the balls to be a dope runner. He didn't like that he was his driver, but his uncle, whom he and Hot Boy worked for, had chosen Hot Boy for the task, so he had no choice…yet. Hot Boy took a deep breath and tried to relax a little. Mario chuckled at him, shaking his head.

"I don't understand why you so scared of the po-lice, though, Hot Boy. They bleed like we do. We do this shit for a living, my nigga and plus, the traps in this muhfucka are dog-proof, no K9 in the world can smell through them."

"Fam, you're *waaay* to calm for a nigga that dun' did multiple bids for drugs and guns, and now, cops dip in behind us when they could've went around?" Hot Boy replied as he rolled under the Canal Street bridge.

"Number one, you don't know that it's the cops, and number two, I ain't no *bitch ass* nigga! *That's* why I'm calm, pendejo! Fuck you mean! Prison ain't shit. I'm the man whenever I'm locked down. This the life we chose to live when we move dope. Every day that we get in a whip with illegal goods, we risk getting' took down, or took out, you dig I'm sayin', G? So, it should be in yo' brain that muhfuckas is out here takin' risks, tryna get rich, *fuck* dyin'! Y.O.L.O., my nigga! Just focus on the money we about to check off this drop and quit actin' like a bitch!"

Hot Boy nodded his head, not even wanting to argue about it any further. "You right, bruh. It's all good." Not wanting to hear shit else, Hot Boy reached over and turned his music up and tried his best to relax his worries to G Herbo's "*OFNG*" as it bumped from the stock audio system.

Mario glanced over at the long-haired Hot Boy, shaking his head.

Pussy-ass nigga, he thought, chuckling again to himself.

As the Dan Ryan Expressway reached the Kennedy and Edens Expressway junctions, Hot Boy heard the roar of an engine over the music. He glanced in his mirror and saw the Navigator jump from behind him, into the other lane, then it flew past him like he wasn't even moving. It shot around him and cut in front of him. Hot Boy tried looking into the SUV as it passed, but the windows were too darkly tinted. He watched as it merged over into the lanes for the Edens entrance lanes, then the driver floored it.

"The fuck is wrong with them, Joe? Aye, you see that?" he asked, glancing over at Mario.

"Nope. What?" Mario asked, as he continued texting someone.

"The cops in that Navigator on some other shit, fam," Hot Boy told him.

"Yo' ass still worried 'bout them? Joe, just fuckin' drive, nigga! If they *was* cops, and they was on us, they would've flicked us! Pull yo' muhfuckin' skirt down!"

Hot Boy muttered a curse under his breath. "Fuck you, nigga!" he snapped.

Mario busted out laughing at Hot Boy, then continued texting. Continuing on, Mario told Hot Boy to hop off at Touhy Avenue when he saw the sign on the side of the highway come up.

"For what? We gotta stay on schedule."

"I gotta take a piss, nigga! *Fuck* the schedule! *I* run this shit! Do what the fuck I said, or I swear I'ma find another driver that actually has balls!"

Hot Boy started grinding his teeth. Mario talked a lot of shit. Sometimes it was cool, but there were times when it was just too much. It made Hot Boy want to shoot him in his mouth, and if it wasn't for the fact that Hot Boy's boss was Mario's uncle, he probably would've already done it.

The exit for Touhy came up a few minutes later. Hot Boy did as Mario told him and turned into a BP gas station on the corner, right off the exit ramp. He rolled around to the rear of the building, parking where the bathroom was.

He was just putting it into park when suddenly, Hot Boy heard the sounds of tires screeching. He looked to his left and saw the same black Navigator that was riding his bumper earlier, skid to a stop just a few feet away from his door. "Shit! Aye, Mario!" he shouted, scared shitless.

-CLICK CLACK-

Hot Boy felt the kiss of cold steel at the back of his head. He froze in fear, tripping hard now. "M-M-Man…bro! What the fuck is you doin'?" he asked.

Mario chuckled. "I told you. I'm tryna get rich, *fuck* dyin, but havin' a bitch ass nigga like *you* drivin' me around, I *am* gon' end up dead or locked up. And so, my friend" he said, with a devilish grin. "You *are* the weakest link…goodbye!"

Hot Boy shouted, "No, bro, wa—"

-*BOCKA*!-

"Shut up, bitch-nigga!" Mario shouted, laughing after putting a single slug through Hot Boy's temple, blowing his brains out of the window.

As fast as he could, knowing the gunshot had to have been heard by people getting gas, Mario flipped all the switches and turned all the secret knobs, unlocking all the trap spots inside the Trackhawk. He got a big, flattened U-Haul box and filled it up with all the bricks, then tucking his switch into his waistline, he looked around first. He saw nobody coming to snoop, which told him that maybe the muffled gunshot hadn't been heard. But still, someone was likely going to ride past and end up seeing the dead man with a hole in his head behind the wheel of the Jeep.

He jumped out of the SUV and hurried over to the front passenger's door of the tinted Navigator. He tried to open it, but it was locked. "Aye! Open the fuckin' door, bitch!" Mario ordered angrily.

The window rolled down just then. Behind the wheel, he saw Julie, a *ridiculously* gorgeous Vietnamese chick that was best friends with his woman.

"Where the fuck is Yvette?" he asked Julie.

She smirked at him, then suddenly, Mario's stunningly beautiful African American girlfriend sprang up from hiding below the door's window line, pointing a Sig Sauer with a silencer screwed into the barrel, right at Mario's face.

"What the f—"

-*PFFT! PFFT! PFFT!*-

Yvette squeezed three silenced shots off, sending each one through Mario's forehead. His head snapped back as the bullets blew a gaping hole in the back of his head, taking his brain with them. He fell to the ground, dead before he landed.

"Come on! Come on! Get this shit and let's go!" Julie urged her home girl, keeping a look out while they handled business.

Yvette jumped out of the Lincoln, grabbed the box and hopped back in. Julie reversed away from the bloody carnage and went around a neighboring Subway restaurant, smartly avoiding being seen by the people that were now surrounding the dead men in the back of the gas station, looking all around for who 'dun it.

***

"Haaaaa! Yeeeaaah, muthafuckaaaa! Bitch ass nigga!" Yvette shouted excitedly as Julie hurried down the on-ramp to the northbound side of the highway. "Always talkin' about '*get rich, fuck dyin*' 'n shit! But guess what, bitch! You *died!* Haa!"

Julie was in tears from laughing so hard at her best friend of twenty years. Yvette was a total nut. She loved the girl like they had both came out of the same woman. Julie was Yvette's bad-ass other half. What Yvette couldn't do herself, Julie *could*. The strikingly sexy Asian woman was a straight up beast in a five-foot-seven-inch tall, hundred and thirty-five pound package. She was aggressive, fierce with her hands, fists and feet, and could shoot the nuts off a squirrel with a pistol from twenty yards away.

Julie, for a Vietnamese woman, had a body. She had hips, tits, and a nice plump round thirty-eight inch ass, along with long dark silky hair that reached down to her lower back. Her exotic looks and her creamy light brown skin and tattoos, could easily make her an *Go Viral* and/or an *Instagram* model.

Her home girl Yvette was five-seven too, with skin the color of caramel, and wavy jet-black ass-length hair. She, too, was tatted up. She weighed just over a hundred and fifty-two pounds, all of it making her *so* voluptuously thick that dicks got rock hard when all that ass she had bounced by them.

The two twenty-seven-year-olds grew up in the northern Illinois suburb of Waukegan. They'd been friends since the third grade. Together, they experienced all of their most memorable firsts with each other, their first crushes on boys at school, first fights, first time smoking weed, drinking and popping pills. They hung with gangsters, hustlers, killers. After they graduated high school, they ended up doing something they *never* thought they'd do.

Yvette's phone vibrated on the center console just then, halting her as she started twerking in her seat. She grabbed it and saw the text from her and Julie's boss. "Uh, oh! Aye, girl, we got another one!" Yvette hollered, looking at the text message she had just received. "Step on it! We gotta switch whips and get to this crash at Route 41 and Buckley Road! Go!"

Julie mashed the gas and swerved over into the hammer lane, stomping it up the highway like there was no speed limit. Knowing her best friend would never get so hyped over something that didn't involve a come up, Julie started grinning hard, *eager* to increase their take for the day.

***

Julie got off of 94 at Lake Cook Road and shot west for a few miles. When she got to the near empty parking lot that she and Yvette had left their vehicle in, she pulled in next to their newer, all-black unmarked Chevy Tahoe and parked.

Julie grabbed the bottle of gasoline and bleach she had by her feet and started dousing the inside of the Navigator. Pushing in the cigarette lighter, she let it get red hot as Yvette hurried to transfer their goods from the Lincoln to the Chevy. Once it popped out, Julie pulled it out and tossed it into the rear row. Flames instantly ignited and grew so hot so fast in the Navigator that as she jumped into the Tahoe with Yvette, it was already a ball of fire.

Yvette peeled off and got her and her best friend away from the inferno. As she rolled back in the direction to get onto the highway again, the two donned their bulletproof vests that had *Illinois State Police* on them, grabbed their holstered Glock .40 service weapons from the center consoles, and clipped them onto the waistlines of their jeans. Yvette then hit the sirens and strobes, flying around traffic. Minutes later, she was back on the highway, speeding north to get to the crash site.

***

Twenty-five minutes later, Yvette arrived at an intersection where Illinois' Highway Route 41 and Buckley Road crossed, up in the Great Lakes area of Lake County. Yvette and Julie saw a number of their comrades were already on the scene. Blocking all access from all four directions were Impalas, Explorers, and a big mobile police command center. State police and Lake County sheriffs were everywhere. Yellow police line tape was up around the area to keep the site contained, around the eighteen-wheeler that had flipped over, after the driver had taken the left turn onto 41 from Buckley way too fast, trying to evade the sheriffs that were on his ass.

Seeing the car-hauler trailer the semi was coupled to had a full load of luxury cars, Yvette and Julie surmised that they were each *fully loaded* models, since the driver felt it was best to flee from just a simple traffic stop.

***

"Evenin', ladies," said Lieutenant Michaels, a thirty-year veteran with the department greeted when Julie parked the

Tahoe next to where he stood by the command center. "You two are just in time. This is a big bust for us. Sheriffs discovered cocaine, crystal meth in ice form, and fentanyl in each vehicle's trunk, in specially fabricated trap spots. The driver is a member of *CJNG*."

"Oh wow. They actually made it to Illinois, eh?" Julie chuckled, having heard about the Jalisco-based cartel, the ones responsible for kidnapping El Chapo's son from a restaurant on his birthday, just to let the Sinaloa boss know that *he* ran the show now.

Shortly after the two turned eighteen years old, Yvette and Julie made a *huge* change in direction of their lives and ended up signing up for the police academy. They became cops after graduating with flying colors. They started off as rookies in the Waukegan Police Department, partnered together after their initial training was over. They did everything from simple traffic stops, house raids, crowd control at political events and festivals. Five years later, they were offered undercover spots in the Illinois State Troopers' *narcotics and illegal goods trafficking prevention* Task Force. The very same day they joined the diverse squad, they had a hand in taking down a big circle of high-ranking players in a major cartel drug bust. Hundreds of millions of dollars in houses, cars, drugs, guns, jewelry and businesses were confiscated. All to be sold off, and/or destroyed...allegedly.

Liking the thrill of being cops, but not liking the chump change they were making, Yvette told Julie that she felt that not every kilo and rubber-banded stack of cash should go to the department, if they were just going to destroy it. Julie agreed faster than Yvette thought she would. Both on board, the two started getting at dope boys and dope girls, taking drugs, guns and money, in exchange for *get-out-of-jail-free* cards, leaving them with no choice but to take the offer...or die.

After the two found *their* in to get more money, Yvette met the nephew of a Colombian cocaine importer, and became the prize he *sooo* badly wanted to win. Yvette did actually like the guy, but she liked the idea of getting rich way more. So, she did what any hood bitch with empty pockets would do. She put the pussy on him so good that he fell deep in love with her.

Over time, she'd been able to get Mario so wrapped around her finger, that when she finally revealed to him that she was a cop, he couldn't have cared less. What he did do, though, was proposition her with big bags of money to watch his back while he moved product up and down the interstates of Illinois. She readily agreed, and got Julie on board, but what Mario didn't know, was that Yvette was already anticipating this. The moment Mario had slid his dick up in her, his life was officially on a countdown.

***

"Yeah. The guys that runs that cartel is probably the smartest I've ever heard of. Hell, he's got the damn DEA scared of him," Michaels said with a chuckle. "Anyways, this is ours since it's involving a commercial truck. The feds tried to swoop in, but I said *eh-eh*! Bounce!"

Yvette and Julie laughed at their boss. He was a polished man of great merit, but when it came down to it, he was still a nigga from the hood.

"Once the two trucks get the rig uprighted and the techs take their pictures, I want you two taking point, get the rig back to the station and log all the drugs you find. There'll be no money and no guns, since that stuff goes *to* Mexico, in exchange for drugs."

Just then from above, the sounds of helicopters came. The three looked up and saw three news choppers hovering. WGN, NBC, and ABC News crews were filming from above the scene, gathering up footage for the evening news.

"Great." Michaels shook his head. "Fuckin' news people get on my goddamn nerves. I'm goin' back to my office. Tran, Jones," he said, addressing the two by their last names. "You two are in for a long night, so I'd cancel any dates you have and grab some Snickers."

"Oh geez, what a shame," Julie said, trying so hard to hide the smile that threatened to rip her cheeks.

"Weeeell… if you say so, sir," Yvette added, feigning frustration. "We're on it, though. You can count on us."

"I know," the lieutenant said, then walked off in the direction that his Ford Expedition was in.

Chapter 2

Around 9:00 p.m., Yvette and Julie had their jobs done. The drugs had been logged in, minus what they had taken for themselves, swapped out with kilos of flour. They'd always been the type to think ahead. They kept plastic-wrapped bricks of flour, crushed glass, and brown sugar close by wherever they went, just for pulling the ol' switcheroo.

They'd taken four kilos of coke, four kilos of ice, and four kilos of fentanyl, wrapping them in the dirty clothes from their lockers and stuffing them into their personal duffel bags. They logged out of their accounts and the two made their way to exit the station. Waving goodbye to their fellow deputies, they'd gotten to the exit door when Yvette heard her name being called.

She and Julie both rolled their eyes at the sound of his voice. Turning, they saw the tall and built white boy with dirty blond hair, wearing a polo shirt with Illinois State Police on the chest, jeans, Nike running shoes, with his holstered service weapon and badge clipped to his waistline.

Yvette loathed the man. To her, he was a whack-ass *Zack Morris Saved By The Bell*-type white boy that had an annoying sense of entitlement that made her want to shoot his nuts off.

"Hey! Jones! Hold up a sec!" he hollered.

"What do you want, Webster?" she asked, not hiding her dislike for him at all.

"I was just trying to see if you had plans tonight?" he asked, with a cheesy-ass grin on his face.

Julie stepped in, pulling Yvette by her waist to her, then made Yvette face her. She kissed Yvette, slobbing her down like a horny porn star that was high off rollers.

Webster's jaw dropped as he watched the two gorgeous women make out right in front of him. They both moaned, their hands grabbing and smacking denim-clad ass. Seconds later, they pulled back and looked at the white boy.

"As a matter of fact, I *do* have plans as you can see, Officer." Yvette told him. "Enjoy your evening. Buh-bye now."

They exited out of the station then, leaving Webster with a stupefied look on his face. Outside, they laughed their asses off as they headed through the brightly lit parking lot, towards where Yvette's 2020 money-green metallic BMW X5i was parked.

"Yo, it's still early, 'Vette. We should go turn up somewhere," Julie said, as they hopped up inside the luxurious beige leather interior.

Yvette push-started the twin-turbo V8 under the hood. "Sounds like a plan to me. I feel like getting' wild as fuck tonight! Oooo! I can hit up T.G. I know he and Bucks gon' be at that new spot. I can let him know we got more product to get rid of!" Yvette told her excitedly, as she pulled out of her parking spot and rolled over to where their Tahoe was parked.

"Yo' ass always on business, girl," Julie chuckled when she came to a stop behind the Chevy truck.

"Hey, what can I say? I'm tryna get rich, bitch! *Fuck dyin'!*"

They both busted out laughing their asses off.

Julie hopped out and got the box of bricks from the Tahoe, then got back into the Beemer truck. Yvette pulled off, exiting the lot with over two million dollars' worth of drugs in her whip. She had no worries at all, though, the state trooper star on her license plate would keep any cop, sheriff, or another state trooper from pulling her over, even if they *did* feel the need to pull over the Black woman driving a newer luxury SUV.

***

In Beach Park, Yvette turned onto Ogden Lane and came to the modest two-story, three-bedroom, two-bathroom house that she and Julie shared. She turned into the driveway and came up to the built-in two-car garage, hitting the remote opener on her key chain. As the door rose up, Sir and Rock got up from lying next to Julie's Fuji White 2017 Range Rover Supercharged, a clean-ass SUV that she had gotten for just twenty-five racks from a police auction, after their squad killed the owner when he opened fire on during a highway traffic stop.

Both one-and-a-half-year-old German Shepherd males ran excitedly to the BMW truck, tails wagging, happy as hell their owners were home. Yvette killed the engine just as a call came through on her phone. "Talk to me," she answered, staying put behind the wheel to take the call.

Julie got out with the two bags. Sir and Rock ran over to her and hyper as hell, hopped on her, yipping and barking at her. "You two need to hush that shit up. We ain't been gone that long," she told them, but relented and gave them what they wanted. Kisses on their noses and strokes behind their ears drove the two insane with excitement.

"Say less," Yvette said, then ended the call. "Aye, JuJu! We got us a job, biatch!"

She got out and grabbed the box from the backseat. The dogs ran over to her and vied for nose kisses and ear rubs from her.

"From yo' guy?" Julie asked as Yvette showered the dogs with affection.

"Yup." Yvette told her what the job was and laughed when her homegirl's face lit up with excitement. "You are a hot mess, JuJu."

"That's my favorite type of job. I can't help it," Julie said with the cheesiest grin ever. "This is gonna be fun as fuck, Joe! On my momma!"

"Yessuh! I'm finna go hop my ass in the shower," Yvette said, then entered their lush home, carrying the box with her.

Julie closed the garage and carried the duffel bags inside, with Sir and Rock trotting along with her. Once she entered the air-conditioned house, she took out her iPhone, went into the iFeeder dog food dispensing app, and pressed feed.

"Go eat," she told them and watched the two run off for the kitchen.

Heading up to her bedroom, she took off her vest, then took her holster and gun off, setting them on the tall dresser. She stripped ass naked and took a look at herself in the mirror.

"Eeeeeee, that's a *baaaaad* ass Vietnamese bitch right there! Look at 'er!"

The tattoo of a heart with wings spanned the whole section of her chest, right above her perky 32 C-cup breasts. The guns, roses, naked ladies were tatted on her arms. On her thigh, a big Vietnamese symbol that said *Blessed*.

She smiled at herself, loving the sexy woman that she saw. Blowing a kiss to her reflection, Julie walked off, heading for Yvette's bedroom.

***

Skip Marley's "Make Me Feel," featuring Rick Ross and Ari Lennox played, crooning from the waterproof speakers around the ceiling of the glass-enclosed marble shower. As hot streams of water rained down on Yvette from the *rain-down* shower faucet, soaking her body, she sang along with the chorus, with her eyes closed.

Just then, the glass door to the shower opened. Yvette opened her eyes and saw Julie had come in with that look in her eyes that instantly made Yvette's pussy wetter than it already was.

"It's about time, *biatch*," Yvette told her, as Julie walked right up to her.

Without words, Julie pushed Yvette up against the wall and started kissing her hungrily. Her hands caressed Yvette's sides, slid down to her hips, then around to cup her juicy ass. The two tongued each other down, heating the shower up even more. Yvette moaned when Julie's hand slid between her legs, fingers entering her, stroking her sensitive walls. She started playing with Yvette's clitoris. Yvette's body shook with bliss.

The two had been lovers for a very long time. They loved men, but they also loved each other. When there were no guys around, they pleased each other, and they made each other cum so hard.

Julie parted from Yvette's lips and started kissing her way downwards. She kissed on Yvette's neck, nibbling at her spot, then continued down, suckling each of her erect nipples. She kissed her way down Yvette's flat toned stomach until she was on her knees, with Yvette's shaved pussy right in her face. Putting Yvette's left foot up onto her shoulder, opening her up, Julie put her face between Yvette's thighs and ran her tongue from the back to the front of Yvette's pussy lips.

Yvette shuddered, feeling Julie's tongue working her. Seconds later, she felt her home girl sucking on her clit. She moaned out in bliss, biting her bottom lip, cupping and caressing her own breasts as the pleasure had her head feeling like it was going to explode. Her moans grew louder, as Julie went in on her. Julie ate her up like she ate pussy for a living. Yvette started trembling and shaking, getting close to climaxing. She cried out, announcing she was about to cum. Julie put her lips to her clit and motor-boated it. Yvette shrieked, back arching up as the vibration sent her over the edge.

"J-J-JuJu! Oooooo! I'm c-cumming!" she screamed out. Yvette exploded in Julie's face, splashing her with her hot sweet nectar.

Yvette *had* to get her some Julie. She yanked her lover up and pushed her front end against the wall. She rubbed and smacked Julie's ass as Honey Bxby's "Touchin' On Me" came on, then she kissed her shoulders, going down her back, down to her ass. With it right in her face once she was on her knees behind Julie, Yvette grabbed her booty cheeks and opened her up.

Julie squealed with delight when she felt Yvette's lips on her asshole. Yvette kissed and licked around the rim of her brown eye. She pleasured it without any hesitation. Julie loved anal stimulation, and Yvette *loved* making Julie cum.

"Oooo, 'Vette! Shit!" Julie cried, rising up on the balls of her feet as the sensation drove her insane.

Yvette licked all up and down Julie's ass crack, before making her way to suck on her pussy. Julie went apeshit when she felt Yvette pleasuring her leaking box. Minutes later, Julie came, squirting all in Yvette's face. Yvette rose up to her feet, spun Julie around, then they made out again, rubbing on each other, jump-starting a second round before they washed each other's hair and bodies.

***

An hour later, the freaky cop chicks were dressed to impress in pricy designer labels, looking *Go Viral* fly. Yvette was in a shiny black Versace leather mini-dress with gold spike studs on the shoulders, a deep plunging cleavage line, a thigh-high length hem, and a gold leather belt around her midsection. She put on gold fishnet pantyhose and shiny black six-inch pumps. She styled her hair up into a tight cheerleader ponytail, gelled her baby hairs down around her beautiful face. After she gave herself *smokey eyes*, and applied glossy red lipstick, spritzed on Versace perfume, Yvette draped herself in gold Tiffany & Co jewelry, flicking so hard. Then she grabbed her mini black leather Versace biker jacket, ready to go turn the fuck up.

Julie, too, was rocking Versace. The top she tied on looked like a narrow strip of black shiny latex wrapped around her breasts. The matching skinny-leg leather leggings were so tight that they looked painted on. She slid her little feet into six-inch pumps of her own, moussed her hair, pulled it up into a bun on her head that looked like a flower bud, and combed down her Chinese bangs. She gelled her baby hairs down around her hairline as well, then put on gold Chanel jewelry, spritzing on Chanel No.5 perfume when she was ready to go.

***

The two sexy ladies got their biggest tote bags from their closets, and each stuffed four kilos of coke, and two bricks of fentanyl inside of them, along with their own personal Glock 21s, and a couple extra clips.

They made sure that Sir and Rock were good with food, water and toys, then together, they strutted out to the garage and hopped into Julie's Range Rover, heading out to a popular club, down in Waukegan.

***

In a plaza on Lewis Avenue, in between Sunset and Golf Road, the humongous building there went from being a big grocery store to *Club 847*. It was the place to be if you wanted to turn up. Gang-bangers, dope boys and girls, killers, broke people, rich people, Black, Latino, Asian, Middle Eastern, and white all flocked to the club to party their asses off.

Julie found a spot and parked. With their loaded totes, they sashayed towards the front of the club, passing by the long line of people waiting to enter. At the front of the club was a group of armed bouncers. The leader of the four was expecting Yvette and Julie, waving them forward when he saw them.

"Uh-uh! Aye! Who the fuck y'all think y'all is?" yelled an ebony-complexioned chick wearing a red faux snake-skin dress, with a horrible looking weave in her head. "Y'all asses ain't special! Rockin' fake-ass leather 'n shit! Get cha'll asses in line!"

"Aye, Yvette!" hollered Tree, as he and his guys hurried over to where Yvette and Julie had paused, looking at the loud-mouth broad. "Chill, lil' mama! Chill!"

"Fuck all that," Yvette said, handing Julie her handbag and walking towards where the girl and her friends were standing.

Julie snickered to herself, already knowing that someone was about to go home with soiled panties.

The girl saw that Yvette was approaching. Not wanting to be punked by a bitch that was shorter than her by nearly half a foot, she stepped out of line, balling her fists up. "What's up, bitch? You want a problem or somethin', Joe?" the girl snapped.

Everyone in line stepped out to see the fight. The bouncers were all halted by Julie when she told them all to fall back and let the shit-talking bitch get some act right.

Yvette said not a word. She walked up to the bitch and ducked the right jab the girl threw, pivoting to her left and following up with a devastating left hook to the girl's kidney.

"Aaahhhh!" the girl screamed, then she farted. Doubling over in pain, her bowels started evacuating. A stream of diarrhea squirted down from under her tight dress, splattering all over the ground and her high heels. Yvette then grabbed the girl's head and rammed her knee up into the girl's nose, breaking it. She snatched the girl's weave out and

21

tossed it, then letting her go, she shot a hard upper cut to the bitch's jaw. The girl flew backwards, landing on her back in the puddle of her excrement.

"*Daaaaayuuuuuum*, Joe! Aye, shortie just did 'dat!'" yelled some guy, while others gasped, laughed and clapped.

The girl's friends were shell-shocked with fear. Yvette looked at them. She told them, "Pick your homie up. She needs a bath and she gon' need some Tylenol." Laughing her ass off, Julie went and took Yvette's hand and ushered her away.

"Aye, lil' mama! Lemme get cho' number!" another guy yelled, but was ignored as the bouncers nearly hurried the ladies into the club, so they wouldn't beat the *shit* out of anyone else.

Chapter 3

Inside the club was live. Flashing lights changing colors every few seconds, a live DJ had the newest music bumping, people were drinking, dancing, balling out of control. Sexy women were shaking ass everywhere, trying to catch something for the night that could give them multiple orgasms, and a few dollars.

As they got to where the bar was, Yvette saw T.G., looking like a six-foot-tall Ferragamo-clad male. Rolling with him, as always, was T.G.'s six-foot-one-inch tall right-hand man, Bucks, sporting an Amiri fit with the Amiri *bone* sneakers. Both men had fresh bald-fade haircuts. T.G. was the color of milk chocolate, while Bucks was a few shades lighter. They were both draped in jewelry that was embedded with flawless diamonds. The two oozed such a hood rich swagger that the women they walked past immediately stopped what they were doing to get a good look at the two, ignoring the guys they were with, or had initially been trying to attract the attention of.

"What up, gorgeous?" T.G. asked, hugging Yvette and planting a soft kiss on her cheek.

"Hey, handsome," Yvette said, feeling shy as hell whenever she was around him. "What's good with you?"

"You," he replied with a smile full of pearly white teeth. Yvette felt her nipples get hard at the sight of his lips.

Julie grabbed Bucks, yanked him closer, and pulled him down to her. He wrapped his arms around her and squeezed

CHRISTOPHER "DIESEL" HORNEZES

her ass as she kissed his lips. She kissed him once, then gave him another and another, before she let him go, smiling mischievously up at him.

"Come on with us," T.G. said to Yvette and Julie. "We got a VIP section from my mans that owns this joint."

***

T.G. and Bucks led the two to their elevated party zone. There were already three more of their homies there, enjoying lap dances from scantily-clad groupies.

"Y'all remember Flip, Low, and G.B., right?" he asked them.

Yvette and Julie nodded, then waved hello to the fellas. The other women, though, were not happy.

"Damn, T.G.!" snapped a dark-brown skinned chick, wearing a blood-red bob-cut wig that matched the skin-tight body suit and heels she had on. "Why is you steady bringin' hoes up in here! You coulda' brought the rest of my bitches up and we all could be gettin' it in right now!"

Yvette's eyebrows furrowed at the girl's blatant disrespect. She took a step forward, ready to whoop her another bitch, when Julie held out her arm, halting her. She leaned in and said into her ear, "My turn," then dropped her bag on the floor.

Yvette's lips curled into a devious smirk as she watched her very skilled friend walk towards the bitch. T.G. and Bucks stood there, not wanting to interfere at all. Hell, they loved seeing Yvette and Julie beat ass. They truly put on a show when they got to thumping bitches up.

"Excuse me, Miss, but would you mind not calling my friend and I hoes? Just because we have high sex drives and we fuck a lot, that doesn't make us sluts," Julie told her.

The girl looked at her other two friends, then back at Julie. The three busted out laughing at her. "Bitch! Be gone before

I trash yo' lil rice-eatin' ass, *hoe!*" the girl said, standing up to intimidate the much shorter Julie.

Julie shot a blow so hard to the girl's stomach that it made her fart. She doubled over from the wind being knocked out of her, then Julie grabbed her and started kneeing her in her gut as hard as she could. The girl farted three more times, then she shitted on herself.

"Eeeeewwww, shit!" Flip shouted, jumping away as a big brown stain appeared at the seat of her bodysuit.

Low, G.B., T.G., and Bucks laughed so hard that they all had tears in their eyes. Yvette assisted her friend, though Julie had it under control. She grabbed the girl's wig, threw it in the face of one of her friends, then grabbed her by what little hair she had and threw her down the steps. The girl landed right on her face. Everyone that was crowded around the steps jumped away, then started laughing and teasing when they saw the big brown bubble at her ass.

The girl's friends were stuck in shock, eyes wide, sick to their stomachs. Julie and Yvette turned and grilled them with venomous glares. They got up and ran for their lives, running right past their shitty-booty friend without even attempting to help her up.

T.G. looked at the puddle of liquid shit on the floor of his VIP spot. Shaking his head, he yelled for a security guard. "Aye, yo! We need a mop up here!" he yelled out. "We got bum-ass bitches poopin' on the floor 'n shit, Joe!"

***

T.G.'s homie gave him and Bucks access to a private lounge area in the rear of the club. They took Yvette and Julie to it for a little more privacy, for business, and pleasure. Bottles of Moët and Ace had been delivered by a bottle girl, along with a big bag of high-grade loud pack and blunts.

Bucks turned on the music system in the room and put it on some G-shit. The ladies sat down on the big leather wrap-around couch, setting their bags on the shiny marble table in front of them.

"So, what we got, gorgeous?" T.G. asked, as he brought crystal champagne flutes over and sat next to her.

Bucks cut the tip off a Cuban cigar. He flicked a Zippo lighter up and started puffing it as Yvette and Julie took all the kilos out of their tote bags.

"Oh, shit! Okay, then! Y'all got some kill bill for a nigga or what?" T.G. asked, liking what he was seeing.

"The coke is *pure* Colombian, no cut at all," Julie told him. "And the fennie is *supreme*."

"How the hell y'all get y'all hands on pure cocaine in this day and age?" Bucks wondered.

"That's not important, boo," Julie told him.

"What *is* important," chimed in Yvette, looking at T.G. as he poured the four flutes of champagne. "Is that we need a buck 'fitty for it all. At these prices these days, *especially* for pure, I need twenty gees a key. That's a deal, it basically makes the fennie free, and I'm still givin' a few bricks away for nothin'."

T.G. nodded his head, then looked at Bucks.

Bucks nodded his head back. "Aight. We'll take it," he agreed.

T.G. took out his iPhone and got right to it. He went into the offshore account that he and his guy shared, wire-transferred the money in full, to the offshore account that Yvette and Julie shared.

Seconds after, they both got notifications of the deposit sent to their own iPhones.

"Now, where were we?" asked T.G., ready to party.

"We were about to turn *thee* fuck up, handsome," Yvette said, as she put her flute to her lips and took a sip, still wearing her flirtatious smile.

"*All* the way up," Julie added, wearing the same smile as she looked at Bucks.

***

"Wooooo shhhhiiiiit! *Fuuuuck*, shortie!" groaned T.G., his eyes rolling to the back of his head as Yvette deep throated his thick ten-inch shaft.

On the other side of the wrap-around couch, Bucks sat with Julie on her knees in front of him as well, swallowing his nine-inch cock.

NLE Choppa's "Make 'Em Say" featuring Latto bumped loudly as the two freaks sucked dick like it was a dick-sucking marathon. Yvette and Julie went hard on the two ballers. Sucking dick was what got them extra horny, wet, and ready to fuck.

Yvette gripped T.G.'s cock with one hand and jerked him while she sucked. Julie used no hands at all while she deep throated him, taking him all the way to the back of her throat. He groaned, cursed, couldn't sit still for the life of him. Julie *loved* it when she made a man squirm from her oral skills. It made her feel powerful.

T.G. watched with glee as Yvette domed him up. His dick pulsated in her mouth, spasming. She released his dick, spit on it, then looking up at him with a seductive smirk, she jerked his cock, making it slick with her saliva and his pre-cum.

Julie got up after she spit Buck's dick out. Bucks got up and spun her around. He untied and tossed her top, freeing her breasts, then he made her bend over, hands on the couch cushion. He undid her pants and rolled them down to her ankles. Her thong was ripped off, then he filled her up with dick from the back. Julie squealed from how thick he felt inside of her.

Yvette let go of T.G.'s cock and stood. She pulled her dress up, dropped her pantyhose and turned around, putting all that ass in his eyesight. She sat on his pole, sliding down on it. She started riding him, reverse cowgirl. T.G. reached up and gripped her phatty, smacking it, loving how it looked as she bounced up and down on him.

The four fucked each other's brains out for nearly half an hour. Yvette climaxed four times to Julie's five orgasms. When T.G. and Bucks got ready to bust their nuts, their ladies got on their knees and opened up wide. The fellas jerked and stroked until they came, nutting all over their faces.

Yvette and Julie started tongue kissing, swapping cum-mixed saliva with each other, putting on a show for the men.

"*Daaamn!*" T.G. exclaimed, astounded by how unbelievably freaky the two were.

"Wow." Bucks was amazed. "Y'all two gon' make whatever niggas y'all end up devoted to some seriously happy dudes."

Yvette and Julie giggled at him, then they got up naked, cum still on their faces.

"I could use a drink, T.G.," Yvette said, smiling at him.

"Me, too," Julie told Bucks.

The guys got the ladies more champagne. T.G. and Bucks powered up, popping ecstasy pills and blowing a blunt of loud between each other, since the girls didn't smoke. Once they were all tipsy and highed up again, they got it in again and kept on fucking each other's brains out until they passed out. Yvette on top of T.G., and Julie on top of Bucks. Worked out and beyond satisfied, the four of them all slept the entire day away.

Chapter 4

The constant ringing of Yvette's phone woke her up close to seven o'clock in the evening. Seeing it was so far away on the table in between the wrap-around, she groaned but got up to answer it.

T.G. turned onto his side, still tired as hell. Julie's eyes opened up when she heard her home girl's voice. Buck's arm was wrapped around her, holding her close to him while he slumbered his away in his sex-induced coma.

Julie looked over and saw Yvette's face screw up as she listened to whomever was calling.

"Okay," Yvette said a minute later, then sighing to herself, she ended the call.

"You cool?" asked Julie.

Yvette looked at her. "It's that time. We need to go."

Julie shook her head. She gently peeled Buck's arm from around her. He woke up when he felt her warm body leave his.

"Y'all out?" he asked groggily.

"For now. We have some business to handle," Julie told him, gathering her clothes from the floor.

Yvette woke T.G. up with a kiss on his lips. She told him she and Julie had to leave but would see him and Bucks another time.

"Hit my line," he said, then closed his eyes and went back to sleep.

***

Yvette and Julie headed home. They cleaned up after their dogs, and then got showered and dressed. Yvette got dressed in an orange, form-fitting, long-sleeved ribbed Gucci dress with a mid-thigh-length hem, brown pantyhose that emphasized her sexy legs, and put on brown suede calf-high Gucci stiletto booties. She grabbed her brown leather biker jacket, put red lipstick on, big gold hoop earrings in her ears, a gold necklace around her neck, then after parting her hair up the right, leaving it to hang loosely, she spritzed on some perfume and grabbed her iPhone.

Julie dressed in a violet-purple tight-fitting Yves Saint Laurent dress with metallic gold strings woven in the sides, long see-through lace-woven sleeves that led to a see-through, above-the-breast line top, and the skirt part of it was leather, stopping at the middle of her thighs. She put on purple pantyhose that had YSL woven in all over them. On her feet, she rocked her new stylish metallic gold Yves Saint Laurent ankle-length booties, which had the letters *YSL* as the six-inch heels. She put on purple eye shadow, glossy purple lipstick, flat-ironed her hair, leaving it hanging loose, then put on gold jewelry, and spritzed on YSL perfume.

From a safe in their gunroom, Yvette and Julie grabbed all the cash that was going to the person they had to go and see, stuffed it all into two duffel bags, then they went to hop into Yvette's BMW truck.

***

Yvette rode out to Lake Forest and arrived at a lavish estate, surrounded by tall wrought-iron fencing. At the main gate entrance, two armed security guards with trained Cane Corsos, stood on point. When Yvette pulled up, one spoke out, using the earpiece in his ear to communicate with the boss.

"Should we have made an exit plan, just in case?" Julie asked, feeling slightly apprehensive by the way the second guard was staring at her.

"Naw. More like we should've brought extra lube," Yvette said.

They both laughed.

The gate started opening. The head guard waved her in. Yvette started rolling, entering the property, travelling up the stone-paved driveway, up to the huge mansion that sat on the other side of a big circular parking section, built with a stone fountain. She went around the fountain and parked next to the new white Lamborghini Revuelto that was parked in a row of all-white foreign and exotic cars. She and Julie grabbed the bags and got out. Under watchful eyes, they walked up to the marble steps and to the giant front glass and gold-framed door.

As they approached it, it began to open on its own. The ladies entered, stepping onto the shiniest white Italian marble floors that covered the entire main floor. They stepped into the big wide open foyer with a high ceiling and a big gold chandelier hanging from it. At both sides, two separate stairways led up to the second floor.

Looking up as the front door closed, Yvette and Julie saw him. He rocked a tight white muscle shirt, white jeans, and white Ferragamo sneakers. His bald-fade was fresh, and his lowly-trimmed beard was razor sharp. The diamonds in his ears, the ones embedded in a long Cuban link chain that hung around his tattooed neck, and in the Richard Mille on his wrist, flickered and sparkled like a bunch of cameras flashing.

He smiled down at them, gesturing for them to come up. Yvette led the way up the left stairway. When they reached the top, they could smell the cologne that the thirty-seven-year-old, five-foot-ten-inch tall Colombian cocaine kingpin wore. "What's good, mujeres?" he asked, hugging them both, his hands immediately reaching back to cup and squeeze their asses.

"You," Yvette said, batting her long lashes at him, giving him a flirty smile. "You lookin' *too* damn good today, Benicio."

"Straight up," Julie added, licking her lips. "You must got a date or something."

Benicio laughed. "I do, I got a date with two of the world's *baddest* bitches. *Goddamn*, y'all look good!" he said, getting a good look at them, loving their tight-ass dresses and that they both had on pantyhose. "Y'all asses be tryna have a nigga dick on bone while I'm tryna conduct business 'n shit!"

Yvette and Julie busted out laughing at him.

"Come on. Sigueme. We got a lil' bit of business to discuss," he told them.

***

They followed Benicio through the vast upper level, out to an expansive elevated upper deck, built with lounge chairs and a couch, a circular fire pit, a big-ass Jacuzzi tub, a bar, with a view of the big backyard behind it.

"Care for a drink, mujeres?" Benicio asked as they reached the seating area.

"Business first, papi. I think better when I have a clear mind," Yvette said, sitting the bags she carried onto the ground, then taking a seat, crossing her legs.

Dropping the bags that she brought, Julie sat next to her and crossed her legs as well. She saw the look in Benicio's eyes as he eyed their legs and thighs. She smiled, knowing that he was craving to dive deep into both of them. He cleared his throat, bringing himself out of his momentary world of lust. He sat down and looked at them for a long minute. They both started furrowing up, wondering why he was just looking at them.

After a minute, Benicio spoke. "My nephew was a piece of shit. He was condescending, and I recently found out that he was snitching," he told the ladies.

Yvette and Julie gasped in shock.

"Mario was snitching? To *who*? *On* who?" Yvette asked, dumbfounded that she herself hadn't known this. "I ran his name multiple times over the period that I had him in my sights for you, Benicio! I swear, neither Julie nor I knew this!"

Julie's mouth hung agape, astounded by the news as well.

"I know, Yvette. Relax. I am not mad at y'all. He was an informant for the DEA. He was snitching on traffickers that worked for CJNG. Y'all heard about that truck that flipped over yesterday? Out in Great Lakes?"

Yvette and Julie both nodded their heads, feeling sick to their stomachs.

"He is the reason the cops got onto the driver," Benicio told them. "Fuck the opps, but snitchin' isn't tolerated, even if it's on our enemies, or competition."

"True," Yvette said.

"Killing his ass was one of the best things you could've done for me," Benicio told her then. "His ass *had* to go."

"I'll admit, I was hesitant to do it," Yvette admitted. "After all, he *was* your blood."

"That bitch ass nigga stopped bein' my family the minute he started ratting people out. Fuck him and his lil' cheesy-ass motto."

The girls started laughing.

"So, no disrespect, papi," Yvette said, "but, when you called, we was a little busy. May I ask why you pushed the meeting up to today?"

"I have a lot of work that needs done, and you two are my golden girls," he told her.

He filled them in on what he needed them for. A few of the jobs sounded crazy as hell, but with the amount of money he was paying for each one…Yvette and Julie were down for whatever.

"You can count on us, baby," Yvette told him.

"We brought what we owe you from the last take, too, Benicio," Julie said. She and Yvette grabbed the bags and set them at his feet. Benicio opened each one up, looked inside and saw all the cash.

He nodded his head, then looked at them. "Keep it, all of it."

They gasped. "B-Benicio…it's three point two million dollars! How you gon' just give it to us like it ain't shit?" Julie asked.

He chuckled. "China Doll, my watch costs more than that. Consider it not only a thank you gift for puttin' that bitch ass rat down, but also the start of somethin' that can have y'all sittin' on top of the world, while still chasin' bad guys and legally / illegally killin' muhfuckas."

"Awww!" they both said in unison. They got up and sat on his lap.

"Anything you need, daddy, you know we got you," Yvette told him, with her and Julie's breasts in his face.

"Yeah, we got you, baby," Julie re-confirmed.

"That's what I like to hear, but now, lemme' *see* that y'all got me," Benicio replied, as his dick got as hard as a steel pipe.

Yvette and Julie exchanged smiles, then they got up off his lap and pulled him up to his feet. And after Julie undid his pants, freeing his hard cock, they both fell to their knees before him, taking his pants and boxer briefs with them.

   ***

"Woooooo, yeeeeaaaaah!" he groaned as his eyes rolled to the back of his head, loving the feeling of his cock down Yvette's throat, while his balls were in Julie's mouth.

On their knees, the two freaks had no problem pleasuring him at them same time. A man that was worth more than half a billion dollars deserved to have more than one bitch suck his dick. Yvette and Julie had no qualms about stepping up and being that for him.

"Shit! Suck this muhfucka, baby! Suck on it like its gon' make you rich as shit when I buss' my nut!"

Yvette released some of his dick and sucked on the head, swirling her tongue around it. Julie massaged his nuts with her tongue while she sucked on them. They had him going insane, toes going wild in his expensive kicks.

Julie let his balls go a minute later. As she rose up from her knees, Yvette gripped him at the base and started deep-throating him again, making herself gag.

Benicio watched Julie go to the lounge chair and climb on, positioning herself on all fours. She tooted her ass up for him and looked back at him, with a seductive smile. Gone by the shape of her perky little panty-hosed ass, Benicio took his dick out of Yvette's mouth and went to Julie.

"Ay, Dios Mio, mira este culo," he said to himself, raising up her dress and gazing at her ass through the purple tights. "Fuck, baby! I love looking at this thing!"

"Fuck looking at it, Benicio," Julie said. "Put that big dick of yours in it and fuck me."

He ripped a hole in her pantyhose and pulled her thong out of her crack. He spread her ass cheeks open and spit a wad of saliva down onto her brown eye. He grabbed his dick and rubbed it between her cheeks, smearing his spit all over her booty hole, getting it all lubed up.

Julie leaned her head down and clenched her teeth when he started pushing the head of his dick into her ass. His size stretched her out, causing her a little pain, but moments after he started stroking her, the pain turned to pleasure.

Yvette went and positioned herself in front of Julie, opening her legs wide for her. Julie ripped the crotch of Yvette's pantyhose, making a wide hole. While she took dick up her ass, she moved Yvette's thong out of the way and started eating her pussy.

Yvette moaned. Benicio groaned. Julie was in bliss.

"Oooo, JuJu! Fuck, bitch! Eat this pussy!" Yvette moaned. Her eyes closed as she focused on how good it felt.

"Yeah, JuJu! Eat that pussy up, mami! Make her cum all in yo' face!" Benicio added, as he kept his stroke game right.

Minutes later, Yvette climaxed, squirting all over Julie's face. Julie licked her clean. Right after, she exploded, cumming all over Benicio's legs.

They switched then. Benicio went to Yvette, slid up in it. She wrapped her legs around him and squeezed her pussy muscles around his dick. Julie sat next to Yvette, opened her legs wide, and let her finger-fuck her pussy.

Benicio went bananas on Yvette, beating the pussy up like he was mad at it. He had her screaming and crying his name until she exploded all over his dick.

Julie climaxed again, drenching Yvette's hand with her hot juices.

"F-f-fuuuuuuck! I'm 'bout to b-b-buss!" Benicio shouted, feeling his nut rising. He hurried and pulled out of the pussy. Yvette and Julie got on their knees in front of him and put their heads together, opening their mouths wide and sticking their tongues out. Benicio started stroking his dick, reaching his nut seconds later. He came all over their faces.

Yvette and Julie put on a show for him after they swallowed what they caught in their open mouths. They started licking each other's faces, slurping up the rest of his jizz, then they swallowed.

"Maaaaaan, oh man, oh man," Benicio said, amazed by the two freaky police chicks. "I think I might just say fuck makin' y'all kill people for me and make y'all my wives."

Yvette and Julie laughed their asses off at him.

Chapter 5

Back at home, Yvette and Julie showered, ate lunch, then got dressed in plain t-shirts, tight jeans, and running shoes. They donned their bulletproof vests and slipped their service weapons into their department-issued holsters and clipped their badges to their waistlines. They went and got Sir and Rock into their harnesses and with their leashes, they headed out, hopped into Yvette's X5i, and made their way to their station for their shift.

For the first two hours, they practiced various training with their dogs. Obstacle courses were first. Then, having aspirations to one day join the K9 unit, they'd been training their GSDs to sniff out narcotics, and bite training. They used real cocaine, heroin, meth, pills, and marijuana. The dogs excelled, finding everything on command, and signaled obediently when they locked onto whatever scent they were seeking out.

"Lookin' good, Officers Jones and Tran," said Lieutenant Sikes, head of the K9 division, as he approached them with his three-year-old Belgian Malinois named Benjie. "I've been watchin' you two, keep it up and I'll have you on my squad real soon."

"That's a big 10-4, *Lieu*," Julie replied respectfully.

Just then, before Yvette could speak, they all heard a call come in on his radio.

All available units! Shots fired at officers! Man down! I repeat! We have a man down! Round Lake, Rosewood

Garden Apartment complex! Armed cartel members holed up in an apartment building! All available units are needed now!

"Let's go!" Yvette said, ready for some action.

She and Julie grabbed their two-ways, got their dogs, and hurried out to their Tahoe. Behind Sikes, they rushed out of the station's lot, sirens blaring, strobes flashing, hearing more distress calls over the radios for back-up.

***

Out in a recessed section of Round Lake, Yvette followed the lieutenant's Expedition into the tucked away apartment complex. Cops were all over the place, tactical response teams and SWAT were already gearing up to go in. Residents that lived inside the building the suspected drug traffickers were holed up in and shooting at whoever came close to the building, had been evacuated and rushed far off to the side, out of harm's way.

There were white shirts gathered up on the side of a mobile command unit, with the leader of the SWAT team reviewing the schematics of the building. Yvette, Julie, and Lieutenant Sikes headed over to be briefed on the situation.

"This is a highly volatile situation, ladies and gents. We've got dangerous guys inside of the building, armed like Special Forces. We've already lost one of ours. There is *no* compassion from this moment on! Shoot to *kill!*" the commander declared angrily.

Suddenly, gunshots from what sounded like machine guns started flying out of one of the apartment's windows. From the window next to it, a firebomb flew out and landed in the bed of a pick-up truck that was parked under it.

The pick-up exploded, causing the cars on the sides of it to blow up. The gunshots flew in every direction. Cars and SUVs were shot to pieces, windows were blown out, people ducked for cover as so many bullets overwhelmed everyone.

"What the fuck are they shootin' up there, man?" Yvette wondered as she crouched down on the side of a marked Round Lake Police Impala next to Julie. "These muhfuckas is *really* on that, Joe!"

Julie didn't hear her, though. Her eyes were on the movement that caught her attention, in the gap between the two rear buildings.

Yvette noticed that her home girl was not paying any attention to the continuous gunfire and firebombs exploding.

"JuJu?" she said, following where Julie's eyes were fixated.

"Look, Yvette!" Julie said, nodding her head in the direction of where she was looking.

A second later, Yvette saw what her home girl was looking at.

"Oh, shit! Aye! This is our chance, girl! Let's get Sir and Rock and get them muthafuckas!" she said eagerly.

"Sounds like another pay day to me, girl! Let's do it!" Julie agreed. Then while the others were still focused on not getting shot or bombed, the two snuck off on their own to get their dogs.

***

"Go! Go! Hurry yo' fat-ass up, nigga! The remote-controlled gun only has five hundred rounds, and the remote firebomber only had thirty fire-bombs! When that shit runs out, the cops gon' figure out that we got little, so we *gotta* get as far away as we can!" Jorge said to Juan, hearing their gun machine and their firebomber still working, as they trudged through the heavily wooded area behind the complex, making their escape from their apartment. "And yo' fat-ass said payin' that nerd muhfucka to build them shits for us was a waste of money!" he added.

"Then what the fuck you kill him for, pendejo?" snapped Juan, tired already and out of breath.

"He was a loose end, stupid! Fuck you think I killed him for?"

Just then, from out of nowhere, Juan was hit hard from behind by something furry. A second after he was taken down to the ground, with sharp teeth sinking into his shoulder, Jorge had turned and came face to face with a leaping German Shepherd, mouth open and teeth bared.

"Oohh, shhhit!" he screamed, then the dog landed on him, taking him down and biting into his left arm, shaking and yanking viciously.

The two screamed in agony, but their screams were barely audible, as their automatic robo-gun was still blasting at the cops. They tried to fight the dogs off, but the more they tried, the angrier the dogs got, and the more powerful their bites got.

Jorge and Juan then heard footsteps. As they got chewed on, they saw two amazingly gorgeous women, wearing bullet-proof vests that said *Illinois State Police*.

"Well, well, well… look at what the dogs found, girl," said Yvette, as she stood next to Julie, both of them holding their service pistols in their hands.

"Rodents," Julie said as Sir and Rock held the two cartel members down on the ground, growling and daring them to keep trying them.

The skinnier one looked up at Yvette and snapped. "¡Estás muerta, *perra*! I swear to God, if you don't get these bitch ass dogs off of me, I'ma put hits on your whole family!"

Julie stepped forward and kicked him in his jaw.

"Shut up, bitch! Watch yo' muthafuckin' mouth! You better recognize that neither one of us are wearin' body cameras, *pendejo*!" she told him.

He and his guy swallowed hard. They both knew that a cop in this day and age without a body camera, was the same as a guy breaking into one's house that wasn't wearing a mask.

"Check it out, you two," Yvette said, then paused to give Sir and Rock the command to fall back. "This is what's gon' happen right now, while you two have a chance to get up outta this alive. I'ma let you up. I know who you are, and I know you got a stash spot. You and yo' fat-ass home boy gon' take us there, we finna relieve y'all of everything, then y'all can go wherever."

"And if I say fuck you, bitch, suck my dick?" the skinny guy asked her, looking at her with a curled-up lip.

"Then, I'ma put the *barrel* of my *gun* in *yo' mouth*, and I'ma make you suck on it 'til it cums all in yo' mouth, bitch ass nigga! What's it' gon' be?" Yvette asked.

"Okay! Okay!" the fatter guy said. "We'll do it! We ain't tryna go to jail! Our boss'll automatically think we gon' rat and put hits on us!"

"Smart man," Julie said.

They pulled the two up from the ground and made them hug one of the trees. They handcuffed their wrists together, stuffed socks into their mouths and put duct tape over their lips. They hurried back with the dogs, realizing that the shooting and bombing had stopped.

Fire crews had put out all the fires. The scene had been contained. They saw SWAT coming out with the remote-controlled weapons that had been positioned to cause chaos from the windows. News crew vans were parked off to the side, reporters were filming the scene, getting live footage for their evening reports.

"Hey, where'd you two go?" asked Sikes, when they walked up to where he stood with three other K9 units' officers.

"Thought we saw movement in the brush behind the rear building, Lieu," Julie told him.

"And Sir hit on something, so we went to check it out," added Yvette, "but it just turned out to be a couple of deer."

41

"Gotta train them to recognize a target versus nature, Jones and Tran. Next time, though, tell someone and take back up."

"Copy that, sir. Was there anyone inside?" asked Julie.

"Yeah. A brainiac that designed weapons for the cartel that the two we thought were inside worked for. My guess is, he was a loose end and got capped so he couldn't talk if caught. There's no signs of the suspects, but we've put their identities out there and once the news shows their faces, someone will come forward and give 'em up."

Not before we're done with them, Yvette thought, keeping a straight face, though her excitement for what she knew was to come was overwhelming.

***

3 Hours Later...

Way past sundown, when all the squads of cops and first responders dispersed, Yvette and Julie stuck around and were of the last to leave. When they got into their Tahoe, they snuck around the rear of the complex, where the woods were, going off road into the darkness. With her headlights on, they came upon where they left Jorge and Juan, handcuffed to the tree. They saw Juan had a huge wet spot in the crotch of his jeans.

"Nasty muhfuckas," Julie said as she cut her headlights off and got out with Yvette, letting the dogs out as well.

They uncuffed the two Latinos from the tree and re-cuffed their hands behind their backs. Searching them thoroughly, they were surprised to see that they were both clean. No phones, no weapons nor drugs. Upon demanding where the stash house was, Jorge told them an exact location. Yvette and Julie then forced them into Sir and Rock's big dog cage in the rear of their Tahoe. They got their dogs up into the rear row, then hopping back in themselves, pulled off to get to where the goods were.

***

Thirteen minutes later, after turning off Rollins Road, down a little street that led to where a neighborhood surrounded a big lake, Yvette saw the house that Jorge spoke of. Surveying the area, the houses around it were either abandoned, or nobody was home.

She cut her lights off and turned into the gravel driveway, rolling all the way around to the back of the house, parking at the back door so that the Tahoe was out of anyone's sight that passed by. Before they got out, Julie grabbed her burner back-up pistol from under her seat. Yvette followed suit, and they tucked them into their waistlines, covering the butts with their shirts.

They got the dogs out, then Jorge and Juan. With their service pistols out, Yvette and Julie followed Jorge and Juan to the back door. Yvette kicked the door open, then she stepped aside, inviting the two men inside.

Inside, Yvette uncuffed Jorge only. He turned on the light, illuminating the dusty basement with spider webs and cardboard boxes all over the place. It smelled old and rank and looked like something out of a horror movie, where a creepy dead old lady would pop out and scare the shit out of you.

Alert and ready to neutralize any threat that came, Sir and Rock gave their humans more of a sense of security.

Still handcuffed, Juan walked in front of Yvette and Sir, while Jorge walked in front of Julie and Rock. Jorge came to where an old washer and dryer were in a corner and stopped.

"Aye, man! Hurry the fuck up!" Julie ordered. "We don't got all night!"

Yvette was ready to let Sir go so he could motivate the man to stop playing games.

"I need a guarantee that you gon' let me and my guy go when we give y'all this merch," Jorge said, looking at the washer.

No sooner than he had made the statement…

-PFFFT! PFFFT! PFFFT!-

Julie snatched out her silenced Sig Sauer and put three in the back of his head, blowing his brains out all over the washer.

Juan's bowels evacuated when he saw his guy's brains blown out. His eyes filled with tears and he started having a panic attack.

"Psssst! Aye!" he heard them yell.

Turning, he found himself staring at *two* silenced pistols, held by *two* angry cop chicks, and being growled at by *two* angry dogs.

"Bitch, you got six seconds to tell us where the shit is, or you gon' look like him!" Yvette swore, pointing her pistol at his throat.

"But with dookie in yo' pants!" added Julie, aiming right at his face.

"The money's in the washer and the dope's in the dryer!" Juan cried as shit ran down his legs. "Please! Don't kill me! Pleeeaaasee!"

"I give you my word, if you're tellin' me the truth, *I* will not kill you," Yvette told him. "Now hurry the fuck up or I'ma shoot your ass in the one that *stink* and *not* the one that winks!"

Julie busted out laughing at her home girl.

Sir and Rock went silent but stayed poised and ready to pounce.

Yvette uncuffed him, then she and Julie watched as Juan waddled past where his dead homie laid on the ground in a pool of blood. He hurried to get all the drugs from the dryer, and the cash from the washer. When he had it all out, stacks of plastic-wrapped tens, twenties, fifties, and hundreds were piled on top of the old washer, and bricks of what they knew was heroin and either coke or fentanyl were on top of the dryer.

"Good job. Now pack that shit up in one of these boxes and hurry up. We'll take you to a Greyhound station so you can get gone, you know what'll happen to you when your boss catches up and you tell him you lost all this merch and let yo' guy get capped."

"B-But...what about my f-family?" Juan asked, looking at them.

-PFFT! PFFT! PFFT! PFFT! PFFT! PFFT!-

Julie squeezed the trigger repeatedly, taking Juan's face off and painting the wall behind him crimson. He fell dead next to his home boy, their blood mixing together, making them blood brothers in the afterlife.

"You was supposed to wait until he loaded our Tahoe to kill him, JuJu," Yvette said. "Now *we* gotta load it."

"It's better than listening to his annoying-ass voice and smelling them burritos he had for lunch. Fuck him. Let's hurry up, pack the shit, and get on. Maybe we can catch a couple of speeders on the way into the station."

They got the money and drugs packed into a box and into the Tahoe, and the dogs were put into their cages. Yvette and Julie then went back inside with long grill lighters and started burning the boxes and paper they found. The fire quickly spread and started burning up all evidence of them being there.

***

They ran out of the house, jumped into the Tahoe and dipped off, leaving the scene unseen by anyone in the area. As soon as they were making the left turn onto Rollins to head back east, they both screamed with excitement, high fiving each other.

"Another one, biiiatch!" Yvette hollered.

"Yeeaaaah, bitch!" yelled Julie as Yvette put a little pep in their step. "We out here getting' rich as *shit*! *Fuck* tryin'!"

The two laughed their asses off as Yvette got them far away from the burning house, with hundreds of thousands of dollars' worth of cartel cash and drugs.

***

Back at the station, Yvette rolled past a few of the third-shift officers as they headed in for rollcall. A few of them that she and Julie were cool with waved at them.

She parked the Tahoe in a space that was just a few away from her BMW truck. Julie got the box and hurried to get it into the rear of the X5i, then covering it with a blanket, she closed the rear door back and went to get the dogs out with Yvette.

Heading inside, they made everything seem normal with them. They chatted with a few officers and a lieutenant. After they clocked out, they got into the Beemer truck and headed home, parking inside the garage.

Before they got out, Yvette made a call to T.G.

"Talk to me, gorgeous," he answered on the third ring.

"Hey, you. I wanna come cook for you. How does fried chicken, corn, and mashed potatoes sound?" she asked him.

"Like you tryna' make me wife you," he replied.

Yvette giggled her ass off.

"I'm at the crib with bro," T.G. then told her.

"See you soon, baby," Yvette said, then ended the call.

Chapter 6

Yvette and Julie tended to their dogs before leaving out. They took them out for a run, fed them stovetop cooked food, then they gave them baths. They then went to shower and get dressed.

Yvette put on a leather Fendi belly-top shirt that had the mini-skirt, mini-jacket, and the six-inch pumps to go with it. After she got dressed, she applied a little makeup, sprayed on some perfume, then iced herself out with one of her diamond necklaces and watches.

Julie slid into a mini shoulder-less red and yellow snake-skin Balmain dress. With it, she put on black pantyhose, and yellow Balmain knee-high stiletto boots. Yvette braided eight neat cornrows in her head to the back and banded the tails at the nape of her neck, then she did her makeup. Julie spritzed on perfume, frosted her neck and wrists out with her own diamond jewelry, then the two took flicks together.

Grabbing a few bricks of coke and tucking them into a small duffel bag, they went and hopped into Julie's Range Rover, leaving the garage and making their way to where T.G. laid his head.

***

Up in Zion, Julie turned into the Stonebridge Crossing subdivision, which sat along the side of Green Bay Road, minutes away from the Illinois-Wisconsin state line. She passed a few of the big luxury homes before reaching T.G.'s driveway. Sitting in it was T.G.'s brand new wide-body Dodge Challenger Demon SRT-170. Next to it was Bucks's Hellcat Dodge Durango.

The two-car wide garage door that was built into the big two-story home was up. Inside, T.G. and Bucks were standing next to their custom painted and chromed out Suzuki GSXR1300's, puffing on loud.

The ladies got out of the Range with the duffel bag and entered the garage. Yvette went to her dude and got a sweet kiss on the lips from him. Bucks wrapped his arms around Julie and tongue kissed her to the point that her knees nearly gave out.

"Damn, baby, you look good than a muhfucka," T.G. told Yvette, taking her hand and spinning her around to get a good look at her in the sexy tight Fendi outfit. "You tryna make a nigga put a couple of babies in you tonight, huh?"

Yvette laughed at him. "I mean, I most definitely wouldn't stop you if you refused to pull up outta this wet-wet."

Bucks and Julie were still slobbing each other down like horny teenagers. His hands had travelled down from her sides to her ass, palming and squeezing it like he was kneading pizza dough. They'd tuned everything else out that had nothing to do with them, until Bucks's phone started ringing from his pocket.

He pulled back from her. "My fault, bae," he told her, pulling his jack out to see who it was that was interrupting their moment.

When he saw it was one of his and T.G.'s runners, he frowned, wondering why the guy was calling.

"Yeah?" he answered, with Julie's arms wrapped around him.

She looked up at him, admiring his strong jawline and his incredibly handsome face. But as she gazed at him, she saw his face go from puzzled, to furious, in mere seconds.

"Aight. Just be cool," he simply said, then he ended the call.

"What up, bruh?" T.G. asked with suspicion, holding onto Yvette's waist.

Bucks looked at him. "We have a big problem, fam."

Closing the garage, Bucks told T.G. what their runner had just told him. Shocked and immediately irked, T.G. started grinding his teeth.

"Ladies, I apologize, but we're gonna have to cut this evening short," T.G. told the two.

"Hold up…why?" Yvette asked with a raised eyebrow.

"Yeah, T.G.! You forgot that we the ones that you *should* have with you on this?" Julie added.

"This ain't no simple bang-bang, JuJu," Bucks told her.

"Not even close to it. It's finna be a gang of these bitch ass niggas there, and they all gotta go to sleep," T.G. said.

"Okay? That's what we do, baby." Yvette pulled him down by the collar of his shirt and looked him in his eyes. "JuJu and I, we lay all types of bitch ass niggas down. We some *bad* bitches wit' gunz, and we licensed to kill. We are *goin'* with y'all. *End* of story."

T.G. started smiling at her. The respect and admiration he already had for her had just grown ten-fold. He looked over at Bucks and saw his home boy smiling and nodding, with a cheesed-up Julie next to him.

"Aight. Y'all can roll…*but*," he paused. "my home boy and I are goin' in first. You two watch our backs and we'll all walk up outta there."

"So, we can get back to enjoying our evening," Yvette concluded with a smile.

"Yup. So, here's how we gon' do this," said T.G., then the ladies and Bucks listened intently as he put a Plan A, B and C out there.

When he finished, Bucks, Yvette and Julie were all smiling their asses off.

"That is some cold-blooded shit, bruh," chuckled Bucks.

"I think I just fell in love with you, Tremaine," said Yvette, calling T.G. by his government name.

"Wait 'til tonight, baby," T.G. told her, pulling her to him and wrapping his arms around her once again. "You gon' *love* the freaky thangz that I do to that ass."

Julie yanked Bucks back down to her and started kissing him again, wildly and hungrily. "I love you, Bernard," she said when she pulled back, revealing her true feelings for the thugged-out dope boy.

"I been waitin' a long time to hear that, JuJu," Bucks said, before planting a kiss on her lips. "I love you, too, baby. There ain't never been another chick that has my heart like you do."

"Aww! Baby, you are so sweet!" Julie gushed with excitement from his words.

"Aight, people!" Yvette said. "Let's make moves. The faster we get this shit done, the faster we get back and get it on 'n poppin'!"

***

Down in Granite City, Illinois...

"Hail Satan!" yelled Pig, leader of a racist mob of devil worshipers that went by the name *Berserkers*.

"*Hail Satan! Hail Satan! Hail Satan!*" yelled just over fifty of his foot soldiers, men and women, all of them with swastikas tattooed on them somewhere, and other symbols of White Power.

In a big farm's barn in the southwestern city of Illinois that they used as their bike club's hangout, the Berserkers were partying their asses off, celebrating a big victory. Big kegs of beer sat on tables, bottles of whiskey and rum were everywhere. Potent weed, cocaine, heroin, fentanyl, and crystal meth was being smoked, shot up, and snorted. There was even a number of women that were either on their knees in front of everyone, sucking dick, or getting fucked.

Death Metal blared from all the big house speakers that Pig and two of his capos brought in from the house that was next to the barn and wired up inside.

"Let's fuckin' party, y'all! We got us a bunch 'a drugs 'fur free off 'a those up-north monkeys! How 'bout that!" Pig yelled to his people.

The crowd all screamed, cheered and whistled. Just hours ago, he and his capos had robbed a Black man that had come from up north to drop off more than a hundred grand worth of goods to one of their associates. They beat the drug runner to a bloody pulp, then they beat the associate up for doing business with Negroes. They took all the merch and dipped to their land where nobody was allowed to step foot on, unless you were a Berserker.

***

Seeing he had successfully gotten his people hyped up and ready to party, Pig was walking off to go to the table where the drugs were, when two blondes stepped up to him, with the most mischievous smiles on their faces. They were both scantily dressed in tiny tops, mini-skirts, and *fuck-me* pumps, with makeup on that made them look like whores from the early 90's Hollywood streetwalker movies. Pig's dick instantly grew hard as he envisioned the little slut-buckets giving him a threesome.

"Hi, Pig! I'm Gwen," the one wearing a denim skirt said, "and this is my girl, Emily." She touched the shoulder of her friend, who had on a tiny leather skirt. "Can we party with you tonight, hot stuff?" Gwen asked.

"Sure, you can, as long as you two are both fans of the red man," he said to them, smirking deviously at the two bimbos.

"Yes, we are! *Hail Satan!*" they both shouted in unison.

"Would you suck the cock of the evil one?" Pig asked them both.

"I'd suck his big red cock in *front* of my husband," Gwen told him.

"Me, too!" Emily added, licking her lips.

"Then come with me, Gwen and Emily, and I will introduce you to him personally. He lives through me, so you will do as I say in my private quarters," Pig declared.

With glee, the two freaks followed the Berserker boss through the large crowd. He led them to where a door was, through it and into a hallway that led to a small bedroom. He took them inside and closed the door, locking it.

He commanded them to get naked, but to keep their heels on. They obeyed him like trained dogs. Pig went and pulled out a baggie of powder cocaine that was mixed with crystal meth in ice form from a dresser. He made them each snort four big lines. They were charged up like he hooked them up to a car battery afterwards.

"Woooooo! Hail Satan!" Gwen shouted, high as a kite.

Emily's pussy dripped from how good she felt from the euphoric bliss making her body hum.

Pig snorted some of the drug himself, then threw his head back, snorting it all down.

The two then fell to their knees before him, sucking his dick at the same time. Gwen sucked his cock while Emily sucked on his balls. After a few minutes, he pulled them both back up and took turns fucking them in every hole that he could get his dick to fit in.

"Yeah!" he shouted as he stuffed himself inside of Gwen's tight asshole. "Hail Satan! Hail Satan! Hail—"

-BOOOM!-

Before he finished his last chant, a deafening explosion rocked the whole barn. The blast scared the shit out of the girls. Gwen's bowels loosened up and she shit right on the floor, while Emily's heart pounded in her chest.

"What the hell just happened?" Pig wondered as he hurried to pull his underwear and his Lee jeans up.

The sounds of machine gun fire erupted right then. The girls, still ass naked, screamed in fear. Pig ran to a metal cabinet and got his tactical-grade Mossberg 12-gauge shotgun out of it. He pumped it and ran towards the door.

"Hey! What about us?" Gwen shouted, terrified beyond belief.

"Come!" He gestured to them to go to him. "I will protect you!"

In their heels, they ran to him, leaving their clothes on the floor. Pig opened the door. They followed him out into the hall, creeping behind him to the door that led back out to the main area of the barn.

At the door, Pig opened it up and saw chaos in the ultimate form. There were bodies on the ground. Blood and guts were splattered all over the place. People were running scared, some ducking. A few were actually shooting back, firing out of the opened barn door, in the direction that the bullets were coming from.

Out in the darkness, Pig could only see the muzzle flashes from the shooters that were using the cover of darkness to hide. Whatever they were shooting was *big*.

"Pig!" shouted one of the Berserkers that was trying to reload his empty .357 Python. "They got Army guns, man! We can't hold out much longer!"

The shooting suddenly stopped. Pig looked out of the barn and saw two figures advancing towards the entrance to the barn. He looked at the table where the drugs he and his two guys had stolen were and cursed. He did not want to leave any of it.

"Girls!" he whispered to Gwen and Emily. "Go! Grab as much of that dope as 'ya can and we're outta here! Do it, and I will personally bless you!"

The girls hesitated, scared to death to move anywhere without him.

"Go!" he urged them.

Gwen and Emily jumped up and ran towards the table.

-BRRRRRRRRRRRRRRRRRRRRRRRRRRRRRRRRR!-
-BRRRRRRRRRRRRRRRRRRRRRRRRRRRRRRRRR!-
More than thirty rounds from the two big guns the shooters had instantly turned the bimbos into piles of blood and guts. Pig cursed angrily at their failure. "Stupid bitches!" he yelled.

The Berserker with the Python jumped up when his revolver had been reloaded and went to fire.

-BOC! BOC! BOC! BOC! BOC!-
Pig saw five red holes appear in the man's chest before he fell to the ground.

Furious, Pig hopped up and pointed his shotgun in the direction of the two shooters that had just entered his barn.

"Die, motherfuckers!" he shouted.

Right as he was about to blast the shotty, the barrel of a gun touched the back of his head.

"Drop it, bitch!" he heard a woman say from behind him, which made him piss in his pants.

***

Yvette put the barrel of the MAC-11 to Pig's head. Julie scooted over to join her, after laying the man with the Python down. She grabbed the big shotgun when Pig dropped it, tucking her MAC-11 and pointing the gauge at him.

T.G. and Bucks had six other men and four women held at gunpoint, marching them towards where Yvette and Julie had Pig held up.

"What the hell is all this shit?" one of them demanded to know.

T.G. pointed his big, fully automatic, military-grade .50 caliber M249 at him and squeezed the trigger. In mere seconds, he was reduced to a pile of raw meat, most of which had splattered all over the others.

Pig and his people trembled with fear. They had never seen anything so gruesome in real life. What had them even more afraid, was that none of the four were wearing masks.

"Anybody else care to ask a dumbass question?" T.G. asked the remaining Berserkers.

Nobody said a thing.

-*BOOM!*-

Julie blew the gauge and took one of the other guy's heads right off.

"Why did you do that?" Yvette wondered, as T.G. and Bucks looked at her with furrowed eyebrows.

"*Because*, I don't like odd numbers," Julie told her.

T.G, Bucks, and Yvette laughed their asses off.

"Hey, man! Look!" one of Pig's men spoke up, hoping to work his way up out of what felt like sure death. "The drugs are on the table! Just take it back 'n let us go! Please, man!"

They all laughed again.

"Well, isn't *this* ironic?" Bucks said. "White man is beggin' *us* for mercy."

-*BRRRRRRRRRRR! BRRRRRRRRRRRR!*-

Yvette put him down with two pulls of the MAC's trigger, opening his chest and his face.

T.G. looked at Pig then.

"For someone that's supposed to be a leader, you sure are quiet, my man. You scared?"

Yvette and Julie looked at Pig. Bucks smirked to himself, already knowing what his home boy was on.

Pig looked T.G. in the eye and defiantly replied, "I ain't never gonna be afraid of a stupid nigger like you! Fuck you, coon!" he snapped, then spit at T.G.'s feet.

Yvette and Julie gasped.

"Ooooooooo...you just killed yourself, dumbass," Julie said to him.

Yvette, Julie, and Bucks then blew the last of the Berserkers away, but left Pig alive...for the moment.

"Kill me too, fuckin' niggers! I ain't afraid to die! Fuck you! Hail Satan! Hail Satan! Hail—"

-*CRACK!*-

Yvette rocked him with her MAC. He flew to the ground, nose broken and gushing blood.

"Shut up, bitch," T.G. said, standing over him. "Trust and believe, you are gonna die, but I got something else in mind for you," he said, looking at the perfect tool of death, laying on the table. "Y'all take this bitch ass cracker outside and I'ma be right there," he then told his homie and the ladies, smiling like the Grinch that stole Christmas.

Chapter 7

"Still not afraid to die, cracker?" Yvette asked, as she and Julie and Bucks stood at his side.

The Berserker boss stood with his hands tied behind his back, and a noose around his neck. The noose was looped up and over a large tree branch, high up from the ground, attached to the back of a custom Harley Davidson, out in the woods by the barn.

T.G. was on the motorcycle, revving the engine up loudly.

Pig's eyes flooded with tears as his time on earth came close to the end, but he still remained quiet, not looking at any of the people that had killed his whole gang singlehandedly.

"Have it your way, cracker bitch," Yvette said to him.

"Go!" Bucks yelled out to T.G.

T.G. kicked it in gear and twisted the throttle all the way back. The Harley shot forward with so much power that when it yanked the thick rope, the noose snatched right through Pig's neck, decapitating him where he stood. His head flew and landed five feet away from his body.

"Whoa..." Julie said, with wide eyes.

"Well, *damn*!" Bucks busted out laughing.

"That's some bullshit, Joe!" Yvette said, pissed off that it didn't work. "His bitch ass was supposed to hang!"

T.G. ran back and saw the aftermath of what he did. "Hmmmm...maybe a little *too* much throttle, huh?" he said to them.

"Maybe just a little," Yvette said, walking up to him, and stealing a kiss on his lips.

"Fuck it. Dead is dead, bruh," said Bucks. "Let's get our shit and get the fuck up outta this racist-ass city."

"Let's," T.G. agreed, all too ready to never find himself in such a creepy-ass area ever again.

***

Waking up to a round of hot wake-up sex had Yvette and Julie in *go* mode. T.G and Bucks put it down. They had the ladies smiling from ear to ear when they were done.

The guys got up and cooked breakfast for them all, then afterwards, Yvette and Julie parted ways from them, going home to tend to Sir and Rock.

***

"Yeah?" Yvette answered Benicio's call while she and Julie laid in her bed, freshly showered and naked, with the dogs out in the backyard running around.

"What up though, mami? I could use a little help if you two ain't busy," Benicio said. "What cha'll on?"

"We ain't on shit, laid up in the bed, watchin' *Chicago PD*. You need us to slide through?" she asked him, as they watched the young blonde chick Hailey Upton get blown back when a box truck full of explosives blew up in a parking lot.

"Naw. I'm in the driveway right now."

"Okay. We'll be right out, papi."

Yvette got up and grabbed her silk kimono robe.

"What happened?" Julie asked her.

"Benicio's outside. Said he needs our help with somethin'. Come on."

***

Yvette hit the garage door opener button as she and Julie exited their house through the garage. As the door rolled up, they both saw Benicio in the driveway, standing between two new Rolls-Royce trucks, both sitting on custom rims.

"What in the world is this man about to have us do?" Yvette wondered as she and Julie walked out to him.

Benicio had a huge grin on his face when he saw the two come out of the garage. He hugged and kissed them both on their foreheads. Yvette and Julie noticed a Maybach truck was parked out on the street. Two women were up front, looking their way.

"Uh…what's up? We takin' a road trip?" Julie asked him.

"You can do whatever you desire in yo' new whips, JuJu," Benicio told her, pulling out the key fobs to the expensive Cullinans. "As long as you make all these broke-ass Lake County niggas 'n bitches look worse than they already do," he added.

They both gasped in shock as they looked at the two Double R trucks. The one on the left was white with a sky-blue interior, sitting on sky-blue twenty-four-inch Modulare rims, fitted with Rolls-Royce center caps. The one next to it was sky-blue, with a white interior, sitting on white twenty-four-inch Modulares, also fitted with Rolls-Royce caps.

"Oh my God… JuJu…this nigga bought us some goddamned Rolls-Royce trucks!" exclaimed Yvette, truly astounded.

"Holy shit…holy shit…holy shiiiiit!" Julie screamed.

Benicio chuckled, loving their reactions. "I gotta make moves, mujeres, but we gon' j-down again soon. Just so y'all know, too, they in a clean name, so nobody tries to link y'all to me."

He gave them hugs and kisses, then hopped into the Maybach truck with the two women and was gone.

Once he was gone, Yvette and Julie stood there for a minute, flabbergasted. They were in such shock that they couldn't move. They were looking at one point two million dollars' worth of SUVs in their driveway that were now theirs.

They both then screamed out at the tops of their lungs, jumping up and down, around and around in a circle, going crazy with excitement.

"*Guuuuuuurl*, when we get off work tonight, we finna pull up on our dudes in these muhfuckas right here!" Yvette said.

"Pull up, pull up, pull up, *pull uuuuuuup!*" Julie shouted, doing a pussy-popping dance in front of her sky-blue Cullinan.

***

Julie cruised in the Tahoe along I-94 heading north. Yvette sat leaned back next to her. En route to head into the station after a long shift, they were happy that they were about to clock out. Plans to see their dudes later on had them geeked with anticipation.

Travelling past Old Orchard, Julie silently sang along with a Moneybagg Yo song, when a Hellcat Charger swerved around the rear of the Tahoe, jumping into the fast lane. The driver floored it and blew past her like she wasn't even moving.

"Wooop! Wooop!" Yvette imitated the sounds of a siren as she reached over to turn on the sirens and the strobe lights. "Get 'em, biatch!"

With the sirens wailing, lights flashing, Julie mashed the gas and made the enhanced engine under the hood roar. The Tahoe shot forward like it was flung from a slingshot.

She swerved over into the hammer lane and saw the taillights of the Charger getting smaller and smaller by the second. She reached out to the dash and pressed a little button that was next to the strobe light switch.

The cold-air boost system was activated and the Tahoe torpedoed from 80 to 110 in seconds. Blowing by the few other north-bound vehicles travelling along, Julie caught up to the Charger very quickly.

Yvette reached over to the built-in computer and entered the vehicle's license plate number.

"It's stolen, JuJu. Chicago has a BOLO on it, the suspect snatched the driver out at a gas station, pistol whipped him, then took the car," Yvette told her.

Julie was just about to speak when suddenly the rear window of the Hellcat exploded from hailstorms of bullets flying out of it. The Tahoe's windshield shattered when they shot through it.

"Shit! JuJu!" Yvette hollered, drawing her weapon.

Julie cursed, ducking down just in the nick of time. Though her foot was still on the gas pedal, the Tahoe started shutting down, due to bullets hitting the grille, penetrating the radiator. Seconds later, the engine died. The Charger got ghost just as they came up on Lake Cook Road.

"Goddammit!" Julie yelled, hitting her steering wheel.

Yvette called the shooting in on the radio that was built into their squad truck. Julie used the last of the momentum to coast the Tahoe over to the shoulder. Coming to a stop, she furiously gripped the steering wheel and looked out of where the windshield's glass once was.

"You okay?" Yvette asked, as reinforcements confirmed that they were en route on the radio.

"Fuck no," Julie growled, then she got out of the SUV, heated beyond belief.

***

Back at the station, Yvette and Julie explained to their boss what had happened. He was livid.

"*Nobody* shoots at my officers for free!" Lieutenant Michaels stated, standing his huge frame up from his big high-backed leather chair. "Soon as we find the cock-suckin' motherfucker, I'm gon' tax his ass all up and down the interstate!"

Too pissed to form words, both Yvette and Julie just nodded their heads.

A knock came at the door just then. Michaels hollered for whoever it was to enter. The door opened up and a computer tech stepped in with a manila file folder.

"Boss, we got a hit on facial recognition," the young trooper said as she walked to the Lieutenant's desk, handing him the folder. "He went to that Speedway on Route 41 and Buckley Road, up in the Great Lakes area, got a pack of Newports and blunts. And sir…he's got a warrant out for failing to register as a sex offender."

"So, he's a fuckin' creep that shoots at my deputies, and he thinks he can just go get high?" Michaels opened the top drawer to his desk and pulled out a bulky .357 Rhino, followed by his back-up Colt 1911 .45 semi-auto. "I'm gon' get 'im so high that his ass don't never come down!"

The young trooper checked on Yvette and Julie, having heard what happened over the radio. They didn't know each other well, but they were all the same age and had been in the academy together.

"Alright, ladies." The lieutenant had typed in the last known phone number linked to the suspect and got a hit on his location. "Our guy's in Waukegan as we speak. I'm seeing he's in a neighborhood called Kirk Park, at a house on Forest and Lincoln. It's the address he used for his parole site, which happens to be where his girlfriend lives." He paused and looked at them. "Leave your radios here, we're going dark for this one. Now, let's move!"

Chapter 8

-BAM! BAM! BAM! BAM!-

"Bitch! Open the fuckin' door!" Wesley yelled out, pounding on the bedroom door angrily.

"Get the fuck outta my house, you fuckin' pedophile!" his now ex-girlfriend yelled back.

Wesley took a step back from the door, pulled out his semi-auto and shot a hole in the lock. He kicked the door open so hard that it almost came off the hinges. The second he stepped in the entryway…

-BOC! BOC! BOC! BOC! BOC! BOC!-

Six shots flew at him, slamming into the wooden threshold. He ducked just in the nick of time before one caught him in his head. Peeking in, Wesley saw Alyssa ducked by the bed that he and she had slept on for nearly a year, before she discovered how truly sick he was.

When she had called to break up with him, she had just learned that his sex case was on a little boy. A little boy that shared his blood. He had sexually assaulted his brother's son, then shot his brother when he tried to murder him for forever scarring his child.

Back before Wesley had been arrested for predatory sexual assault, in which he had told Alyssa that he was charged with plain sexual assault, he told her that the state of Illinois had charged him with it because he had been having sex with a girl that was a year younger than him, when he was eighteen years old. She believed him and seeing that so many other women out there had been and were in relationships with older men, and vice versa, she decided to give him a chance.

When Wesley got the call from Alyssa, she told him that she was done with him and that she was telling his parole officer that if he came back to her house, she was calling the cops on him. At the time, Wesley had been down in Chicago, looking for a quick come-up that he could get on with. Having taken the Metra down to the city, he'd been on foot. He'd stumbled upon a Hellcat sitting at a pump at a gas station while he strolled, looking for a ride to peel and fly back to Wauk-Town.

He caught the driver lacking, snatched him out from behind the wheel, and with his pistol he beat the man, then jumped in and sped off. On the highway, a cop in an SUV tried to pull him over. Refusing to let anything stop him from getting to Alyssa and choking a booger out of her ass, Wesley shot at the cop through the rear window of the car, stopping the SUV from pursuing him.

When he got to Alyssa's house, Wesley barged right in through the front door and caught her riding the dick of a guy that was sitting on the couch in her living room.

Alyssa jumped off of him, falling backwards to the floor. The guy wasn't fast enough, though. Before he could even attempt to run when Wesley pointed his Glock at him, Wesley put one in the center of his face, then popped his ass twice more in the head.

Alyssa managed to make it to her room, narrowly escaping the bullets Wesley fired at her. She closed the door and locked it right before Wesley could get to her, but he had absolutely no intentions of leaving until he taught her a lesson.

***

"Wesley! Get ooouuuut! It's fucking over!" Alyssa screamed, holding up her Smith & Wesson M&P Shield 9mm to fire at him again.

Wesley stood at the side of the doorway, letting her shoot and waste all her ammo. He counted each shot and when he heard the gun click empty, he rushed into the room, jumped over the bed and dove on top of her as she started rising up from her crouched position.

Taking her down to the ground, Wesley grabbed her by the throat and started squeezing, choking the life out of her. Frantically, Alyssa tried prying his hands from her throat, but he was just too strong and too angry.

"Now what, bitch?" he yelled, spittle flying from his mouth onto her face. "You thought you could leave me? Huh? Yo' ass in here fuckin' another nigga 'n shit! You see what you made me do?"

Alyssa couldn't talk, nor could she breathe. Her vision was getting blurry. The light was getting dimmer by the second.

"You want dick, hoe? I got some for you!" he told her.

Wesley forcefully flipped her over onto her stomach and yanked his pants down, freeing himself. Without even a second thought, he rammed his dick into her asshole, penetrating her. Alyssa screamed in agony from the pain. Wesley held her down under him with the weight of his body as he anally violated her.

"Yeah, bitch! Talk shit now!" he dared her, thrashing her relentlessly.

She was in so much pain that she felt close to blacking out. She cried, begging and pleading for him to stop, but he refused. In fact, every time pleaded for him to stop, he seemed to get rougher.

Getting angry at once again, being some guy's poor helpless victim, Alyssa quickly thought up a way to get out from under him. She clenched her teeth, and she started pushing, as hard as she could. In about a minute of pushing hard, she managed to make her bowels explode.

Liquid feces spewed out of her all over his crotch. Wesley felt it, then smelled it. He shrieked, jumping out of her and looking down, he saw his whole crotch was covered with shit.

"What the fuuuuuck?" he roared angrily.

Alyssa hurried and jumped up, then took off running from him, screaming for help. Wesley got up and yanking up his pants with a shitty dick, he chased after her.

***

She heard him coming as she made it to the front door. As fast as she could, she unlocked the door and snatched the door open, just as he jumped from the fifth step to the main floor. She ran out of the house right before he could grab her by her hair. Naked and smeared with blood, Alyssa hauled ass out of her house, screaming and crying for help at the top of her lungs.

***

Wesley went to run out of the house to catch her before the neighbors could call the cops. He got one foot out of the door, when seemingly out of nowhere, a metal pipe came flying, smacking into his right left knee, obliterating it. He screamed in pain, falling forward, gripping his busted knee. Wailing and crying in agony, Wesley held his knee tightly, never having felt such pain in his life before.

A pair of steel-toe boots came into his view a second later. He looked up and before he could see the face of the person standing above him clearly, the tip of one of the boots kicked him in his jaw, sending him right off to la-la land.

***

"Hey! Ma'am! Please, relax! We're Illinois State Police Officers!" said Yvette to the woman, as she and Julie caught her when she ran out of the house.

Right then, they all heard the loud crack. Looking over at the porch, they saw Lieutenant Michaels had just busted the man's knee that they were looking for. Then their boss kicked him right in his jaw, knocking him out cold.

Alyssa calmed down when she saw the ladies produce badges. Their bulletproof vests with their division embroidered on them helped as well. Yvette and Julie took the battered and violated woman to where her and Julie's loaner Crown Victoria was parked, right behind their lieutenant's Expedition.

Lieutenant Michaels ignored Wesley's crying and pleading for a hospital. He cuffed the guy up and took him to his SUV, tossing him in the back where the steel cage was.

All the ruckus got the attention of the neighbors. A few squad cars from Waukegan P.D. pulled up to assist, and an ambulance arrived behind them.

Yvette was able to briefly interview the young girl, getting crucial information on Wesley, before the EMTs took her away to the ER to be treated.

***

"We got him, officers," Michaels told the six uniformed Waukegan cops. "We've been looking for Mr. Coals. He's one of our top confidential informants, he's been missing in action, ever since he fed us a bunch of false information. Now, we need to go have a little chat with him."

The senior officer amongst them nodded his head, happy to not have to do any paperwork before the end of his shift. "Sure thing, Lieutenant. You all have a safe rest of shit," he said.

He and his officers got into their squads and left without another word.

Once they were out of sight, Yvette, Julie, and their lieutenant assured the people that were still outside watching, that Alyssa was going to be fine, physically at least. They also told them that her creep ex-boyfriend was going to be extradited back to California, to face sex assault charges.

Satisfied with that, they all retreated into their homes. Yvette and Julie got into their Crown Vic and followed Michaels in his Expedition, out of Kirk Park and out of Waukegan, heading west, to where nobody would be able to hear Wesley scream.

***

"Nooo! Nooo! Noooooo! Pleeeeaaaase!" cried Wesley, stretched out and ass-naked, hands tied with a rope to the bumper of Yvette and Julie's Crown Vic, while his ankles were bound with a rope that was tied to the back of Michaels's Expedition.

To the side of him, the Lieutenant and the ladies stood, listening to him beg. Out in farm country, they allowed him to scream and yell as loud and as much as he wanted. There was nobody around for miles in all directions.

"Shut the fuck up, bitch! Stop cryin' like a bitch and take this shit like the bitch you are!" Yvette shouted.

"Yeah, *biiitch*!" Julie added.

Michaels laughed at the two.

"So, Mr. Coals." He stepped up to Wesley, holding a TASER in his hands. "You think it's okay to put your dick inside of kids, huh? You think that's a cool thing to do?"

"I didn't do that shit! She lyin', man!" Wesley cried.

Lieutenant Michaels put the TASER to Wesley's dick and zapped him.

"Aaaahhhhh!" he screamed as it made his balls feel like they were on fire.

Michaels let off the trigger. "Answer my question, perv. You think it's okay to have sex with kids?"

"Nooooo! Nooo! I don't!"

"Then why did you do it?" the lieutenant asked.

"I...I...I'm sorry!"

Michaels looked at the ladies. Yvette stepped up with a can of homemade liquid in her hands. She opened the top and dumped the liquid into his face. Wesley screamed when the habanero pepper juice and bleach mixture got into his eyes. He thrashed around violently as the liquid fire ate his eyeballs. The three watched him go berserk.

"Damn. That's some strong shit you made there, young lady," Michaels said with a chuckle.

"Perfect to torture a bitch," Yvette told him.

Julie took out her non-department-issued .22 revolver and gave Wesley the most painful sex change ever.

Michaels then tazed his face, adding to the agony. Yvette poured the last of the liquid onto where his dick had been. It burned him so much that they could actually hear the sizzling sounds.

"Okay. Time to wrap this up, ladies," said Michaels. He went and got into his truck and put it in drive. Yvette and Julie stepped back a few feet. Michaels started rolling forward. The line that had Wesley stretched out got tighter and tighter. He screamed louder and louder, as he felt himself being stretched further and further. In another five seconds, Michaels floored it and pulled Wesley apart at his hips.

The girls looked at the two pieces of creep before them, blood gushing out of both ends.

Michaels came back and looked at the two pieces as well. "I'd love to let him be vulture food, but we gotta bury him. After that, take a few days off," he told them. "Paid, of course. I'm taking off, too. I need some time with the wife and kids."

Yvette and Julie nodded. Their boss got the three shovels out of the back of his Expedition, a tarp, and a can of gasoline. They all dug a hole deep enough that no animal would be able to dig back up, then they rolled Wesley up in the tarp like a blunt, tossed it down into the pit and lit him up. After he burned for nearly ten minutes, they covered the hole up and dragged tree branches all over it, to make the ground look undisturbed.

Bidding their lieutenant adieu, Yvette and Julie hopped into their Crown Vic as Michaels got into his truck. They all crept out of the forest and back onto the road, unseen by anyone that was still out and about.

Chapter 9

Two Days Later...

Yvette and Julie laughed their asses off at what they had just witnessed on the TV. As they were watching the presidential debate, being held out in Butler County, Pennsylvania, someone had taken a shot at the former president of the United States. But, they missed, hitting him in his right ear.

"*Heeeeell naw*!" Julie laughed so hard that tears ran down her face. "Aye! His ass almost just got *got*!"

"Whoever did that sucks. How the fuck do you miss? Dude got a big-ass head and an even bigger mouth," Yvette said, shaking her head as the so-called Secret Service rushed in to "*do their job*.

"I bet that shit ain't real," Julie then said. "What chu' wanna' bet that it was a high-velocity paint ball instead of a real bullet. Weeks from now, ain't shit gon' be wrong with his ear, no scar, no nick, nothin'!"

"And no win, either," Yvette said, damn sure that it was a hoax just to make people feel sorry for him and vote. "Dumbass cracker caught all them charges, got convicted, got people pissed off, then gets nicked in the ear. People gon' be all on his dick now."

Julie busted out laughing again.

The news continued shooting the dramatic scene. The former president was carted off the stage, but before he exited completely, he held his fist up and chanted, *"Fight! Fight! Fight! Fight! Fight!"*

"Shut up! Shut up! Shut up! Shut up, biiiiiitch!" the two yelled together.

Laying by their feet, Sir and Rock grunted from them yelling. They closed their eyes back and attempted to go back to sleep, when Yvette's iPhone dinged.

She grabbed it from the table and saw a message from *"HE."*

"We got some work to do, JuJu." Yvette opened and viewed the message sent by Benicio. "Ooooooo! Look at this!"

Julie leaned over and took a look. Her eyes lit up like lights on a Christmas tree when she saw what the job was.

"I don't think we ever did anything like that before," she said to Yvette.

"Nope. Hmmmm...I *am* hungry, too," Yvette said with a chuckle. "How about a bite to eat, sexy Vietnamese girl?"

"I got somethin' for you to eat, sexy Black queen," Julie flirted.

"As soon as we get back, it's on. Let's go handle this."

Julie nodded. "Let's."

***

"Wow!" the waiter at the front of the big Mexican restaurant said, when he saw the two beautiful women enter the popular eatery.

They looked like video vixens to him, with their hair styled up, makeup and nails done, wearing sexy leather dresses, pantyhose, high-heels, and with a strong gust of wind blowing in through the door when they opened it, he could smell their perfume.

They both walked up to him, with smiles on their faces.

"H-hello, ladies...um...I'm Rafael, and...welcome to *Fernando's*. Dinner for two?" he asked them.

"Yes, please," the Asian girl said to him, with a smile full of pearly white teeth.

He had seen many Asian women before in his life, but the girl in front of him was beyond gorgeous. He loved the heart with wings tattoo that spanned the width of her exposed chest, and the tight dress she had on revealed that she was curvy, compared to how most of the other Asian women he'd seen were very thin.

He glanced at the light-skinned girl. He was sure she was Black, or at least mixed with Black. He couldn't help but allow his eyes to travel down, taking in her big breasts, slim waist and wide hips. He could tell she had a phat ass, and he *loved* it when women wore pantyhose.

"Okay. R-right this way, ladies," Rafael then said, grabbing two dinner menus, two dessert menus, and drink menus.

He led them through the big restaurant, to where a table that had been just cleaned off had a window next to it. Taking their drink orders after they sat down and placed their designer handbags on the table, he headed to go fill their orders. On the way, he made a pit stop where his home boy was frying up some seasoned chicken in a skillet.

"Aye, Dorian, these two badass hoes that just came in, I sat 'em in my section! *Fam*! We *gots* to get at them! Straight up, these bitches are bad as *fuck*, Joe!"

Dorian chuckled. "Make it happen, bro. I got plenty of party favors at the crib."

"Bet," Rafael said, dapping his guy up.

***

Making his way back to serve the ladies their drinks, Rafael contemplated what he was going to say in order to spark up some conversation, when he saw his boss, the owner of the restaurant, at the table where the two beauties were. Right away, Rafael knew that Fernando was doing his *Hugh Hefner* thing, by the way the women were laughing.

Fernando was a very wealthy man, and had the looks that got him any woman, or *women*, that he wanted. Rafael cursed under his breath, knowing the boss was about to cock-block.

Mustering a smile as he approached the table, Rafael put the ladies' drinks in front of them. Fernando was cracking up at some old tired-ass joke. The girls were laughing right along with him.

Bitch-ass creep! They don't give no fuck about a damn thing you're sayin', bitch! If you ain't have that watch on yo' muhfuckin' wrist, you wouldn't be shit! I should take that muhfucka and go pawn it! Rafael thought, as he glanced at Fernando's vintage gold 1969 Cosmograph Daytona Rolex flickering from the light glinting from it.

"That'll be all, Rafael," Fernando said dismissively. "Get back to the front for more guests, young man. It'll be a very busy night. Ladies? Where was I?"

"You were going to show us that old painting you say you have, Mr. Baez," Rafael heard one of the women say as he walked off, salty as hell.

More like he was about to take y'all back to his office and let you dumbass hoes take turns deep-throatin' his tiny-ass dick! Rafael thought, seething with anger that he had just missed out on the opportunity to bag the bitches, because his money wasn't up.

***

One Hour Later...

"Nigga, you really mad right now? Over some pussy?" Dorian asked, seeing Rafael's face all screwed up while he was cleaning his area.

"That old-ass man be cock-blocking, fam. I hate that shit. Think 'cause he got a little bit of money that his ass can take all the hoes 'n shit."

"Yo' ass tweakin, Joe. Number one, you really sound like a hater," Dorian replied, keeping it straight up and down with his homie. "And number two, we got so many bitches on both of our phones that we could call any one of them and they finna come through and buss' down. Let the old man get his dick wet 'cause soon, it's gon' shrivel up anyways."

Rafael shook his head, not really wanting to hear it. "I should kill him and take his watch."

"Wow. Rafie, bro, chill. You do remember that Fernando's cartel, right? Muhfuckas touch him, they asses are grass."

Just then, the smell of meat cooking began filling the air. They looked around the kitchen but saw nobody was cooking.

"Who the fuck is cooking?" Rafael asked with puzzled brows.

"I don't know, but that shit smell *fi'*!" Dorian chuckled. "Smells better than everything *I* cooked tonight!"

No stoves were on, no microwaves, and no ovens were on. The two other chefs and the three cold preppers were on the other side of the kitchen, chatting amongst themselves. Rafael and Dorian were puzzled as to where the smell was coming from.

The fire alarm started blaring just then.

"Oh shit! Aye! What the fuck is goin' on, dog?" Rafael asked, looking around more frantically now.

Smoke then started filling the kitchen. Two other workers that had not been in the kitchen ran in, screaming with panic that the boss's office was on fire.

Rafael hurried to grab a fire extinguisher, then followed Dorian as he ran towards Fernando's office.

The smoke in the hallway was so thick that they could barely see where they were going, and it became increasingly hard to breathe.

Bending the corner, they saw the flames at their boss's door. The two ran to it, yelling for Fernando to holler out. Dorian mustered up all his strength and delivered a hard police-quality kick to the door. It flew open and the flames shot out, nearly frying him.

Rafael started spraying the extinguisher into the office, hitting everywhere that he could until he managed to put the flames out minutes later. When the fire was out, the office still smoldered. Everything inside of it was charred like ruined barbecue. The smoke was still thick and hazy. The others in the crew stood in the hallway, a few feet behind Rafael and Dorian.

The two stepped foot inside to see what they heck had been burning. When they saw where Fernando's chair was, they both gasped in shock when they saw his fried corpse, nearly melted to the chair.

"Holy shit," said Rafael and Dorian in unison, as they looked at what would give them nightmares for the rest of their lives.

***

Turning into a dark parking lot of a dog-exercise area, just outside of Libertyville, Yvette rolled her new Rolls-Royce truck towards the gleaming white 2-door Mercedes-Benz S650 AMG Maybach, sitting in between two white Mercedes G550s.

She came to a stop in front of the Cabriolet Benz and parked, rolling down her window as Benicio hopped out from behind the wheel and walked up.

"Howdy, sir," Yvette said to him.

"Why, hello, beautiful lady. This a nice-ass truck you got here," Benicio told her.

Yvette and Julie chuckled.

"Mine's better," Julie told him.

"Whatever," said Yvette. "We got somethin' for you, though, papi."

Julie held up the gold, one point two million-dollar Rolex with a smile on her face.

"I see a very bright future for the two of you," Benicio told them, as Yvette handed him the watch. "Until next time, beautiful ladies."

With that, Benicio hopped back into his drop-top and pulled off, with the G-Wagons full of his armed goons following.

"Where to now?" Julie asked, as Yvette made a U-turn and headed to exit the lot.

"Dickville," Yvette told her, then called T.G. up.

Chapter 10

The following day, close to early evening, Yvette and Julie left T.G. and Bucks, feeling so very satisfied and worked out. They hopped into Yvette's Cullinan and headed home to get ready for their shift.

***

Throughout the night, Yvette and Julie took turned flagging down speeders on the highway that they mostly patrolled, giving mainly warnings. Other than that, it'd been a quiet night.

Around 2:00 a.m., a couple of hours before the end of their shift, Julie's stomach rumbled with hunger. Deciding to go get some food, Yvette and Julie agreed to go to the restaurant inside the big TA Travel Plaza truck stop on the side of I-94 and Russell Road, at the Illinois-Wisconsin border.

Pulling into the big non-commercial vehicle parking lot, Julie saw that not many people were there, but she and Yvette could see that the truck parking section that was behind the TA was filled with big rigs.

She parked and she and Yvette got out, making their way inside, cutting to their left through the store area, to where the restaurant was. They ordered cheese-steak hoagies, fries and pops, paid for them, then went to sit down at a booth table with a window. They smashed the delicious truck-stop food and left a tip for their server.

They both made a quick pit stop to the bathroom, then were walking past the section where the diesel maintenance and repair garage was, when they heard a scream. Quickly about-facing, they made their way to the entrance door, for it led out to the truck parking lot. They stepped outside into the cool breezy night and looked around. All they heard was the sound of diesel engines idling.

No drivers were out and about, not a single truck was moving, and none had their lights on. Only the tall light poles situated around the lot provided enough light to see.

They stood where they were for a minute, listening, but still had heard nothing other than trucks idling. Shrugging it off, Yvette and Julie turned around to go back inside, when suddenly, they heard the scream, way more clearly.

"Heeelp! Heeelp meeeeeee!"

They drew their weapons and flashlights, then crept fast towards where the scream was. Approaching a row of rigs, they started yelling out.

"State Police! Call out to us!" Yvette hollered.

Just then, they heard the sound of an engine revving up, right before they saw a woman run out from between two rigs, naked, bloody, battered, and terrified.

"Heeeeeeeelp!" she again screamed, running towards them.

"Hey!" Julie shouted, pointing her gun in the direction that the girl had come from. "Come to us! We're cops! We got you, ma'am!"

Yvette caught the girl and pulled her behind her, in case someone was chasing her.

"What happened to you?" Julie asked the girl, knowing that whatever happened was bad...really bad.

Before the girl could answer, a semi-truck tore out of a parking spot, pulling a dry-van box trailer behind it. Hanging out of the passenger's window was a Hispanic man, and in his hands he had an AK-47.

"Gun!" Julie yelled and dove out of the way as the man opened fire.

Yvette pulled the girl to her and dove with her to the ground, narrowly escaping the bullets flying from the chopper.

Julie tucked herself into a ball and popped back up like an acrobat. She immediately started firing at the truck's passenger side as the driver sped off, maneuvering the long rig like a true pro.

The window on the side of the sleeper then was blown out and the barrel of another AK stuck out, spitting lead at her.

"Call it in, Yvette!" Julie yelled, fearlessly taking off after it, while still exchanging gunfire with the shooters.

"JuJu, wait!" Yvette shouted back, but Julie was already gone.

***

-BRRRRRRRRRRRRRRRRRRRR!-
-BRRRRRRRRRRRRRRRRRRRR!-

"Back up, bitch!" shouted Rolando as he blew his AK-47 out of the passenger's window, dumping at the cop chick on foot that was pursuing him and the other three inside of the Freightliner.

The driver, called Trucker, did his best to get the rig in the direction of the exit, but there were so many turns he had to make since there were so many trucks in the lot that had made their own parking spaces, blocking the normal way out.

Back in the sleeper area, Prieto fired his AK out of the passenger's side sleeper window, trying to hit the cop bitch as well. Next to him was Caballo, holding onto his own chopper, waiting for his opportunity to let his K loose.

-BOC! BOC! BOC! BOC! BOC! BOC! BOC!-

Shots fired from the cop flew through the sleeper's wall. Prieto came so close to taking one in his face. More shots were fired, but these ones didn't hit the truck.

The next thing they knew, the truck had drastically lost speed. Trucker and Rolando saw bright sparks in the passenger's side mirror. The shots had blown out the tires on the passenger's side.

"Fucking bitch!" Rolando roared as the trailer's bare rims grinded on the ground.

"We can't drive outta here in this, Ro!" shouted Trucker, as he slammed on the brakes.

"Fuck it! Everybody out! Kill that cop bitch and anybody else that tries to help her!" Rolando ordered.

The four of them hopped out the rig with their choppers and went looking for the bitch.

***

-BOC! BOC! BOC! BOC! BOC!-

Seeing the men jumped out of the truck after she'd blown the trailer tires out, Julie fired more from under a flat-bed trailer that was close by. She heard one of the men scream in pain then hit the ground, grasping at his leg.

The other three turned in her direction, one of them yelled that she was under the trailer, then they started firing.

***

"Aaaaaaahhhhhhh, motherfuuuuuckeeeerr!" Caballo cried as a bullet slammed into his right calf, blowing it completely out.

"Aye! She's under that trailer! Get her!" Rolando pointed and yelled.

Rolando, Trucker, and Prieto turned their choppers in the direction they'd seen the muzzle flashes come from and squeezed their triggers. They each sent more than twenty shots at where she had popped Caballo from.

Rolando yelled for them to halt fire. He ordered Trucker and Prieto to go check it out to see if they'd gotten her.

Trucker and Prieto ran to do as told while Rolando helped Caballo up.

As they came up on the truck the cop had been hiding under, the driver jumped out of the cab, scared shitless. They pointed their AKs at the man and went to pop him, when two shots rang out.

A second later, Trucker's face was covered with Prieto's blood and brains when they flew out of a hole on the right side of his head from the gaping wound made by one of the gunshots.

The petrified driver used the opportunity and took off running while Trucker was distracted.

Stuck in a state of shock, Trucker looked down at his dead comrade, laid out on the ground, with blood leaking from the hole.

"Fuck this! I'm out of here!" the trucker declared.

He jumped up into the rig that scared driver had jumped out of and starting the engine, he slammed it into gear, released the brakes, and mashed the gas pedal. The Peterbilt shot forward and he whipped it out of the parking spot, scraping the truck on its right as he tore out of the parking spot. Speed-shifting gears, Trucker cared about nothing, nor nobody else but getting the hell up out of there. He saw Rolando and Caballo on his right but had no plans on stopping...at all.

***

"Aye! Trucker! Truuuckeeeerrr!" yelled Rolando, as he tried to carry Caballo with him towards where he *thought* Trucker would stop and pick them up.

Then, from a dark cut between two semis, he saw the lady cop run out and get to dumping at the fleeing rig.

"Get her, bro! Shoot that bitch!" Caballo struggled to say, as he grew weaker by the second from losing so much blood.

Rolando sneered. He let Caballo go and took aim at the cop chick with his chopper, while she continued firing at the truck Trucker had stolen. Six shots later, the rig suddenly veered out of control and slammed into a tanker trailer, exploding into a giant ball of fire.

"Fuck!" Rolando cursed, sure that Trucker was dead.

"Ro! Shoot her!" Caballo again urged, seeing the chick standing there, yelling into a phone.

Rolando pointed his gun at the girl, wrapping his finger around the trigger. He clenched his teeth and prepared to blow her away, when suddenly…

-*CRACK!*-

"Aaahhhh, fuck!"

He heard the sound of bone breaking, followed by Caballo's scream. He turned to see Caballo on the ground, holding a gaping wound in his head that spewed blood.

The cop chick that he had forgotten about stood just feet away, pointing her Glock at him. "Drop it, bitch nigga!" she ordered.

"Okay! Okay! Don't shoot!" Rolando pleaded, lowering his weapon. "Look! I got money! Big money! Lemme' skate and I got you! For real!"

The cop smirked at him, chuckling. "No body cam," she said to him.

Rolando cursed when she raised the gun up a little more.

-*BOC! BOC! BOC! BOC! BOC!*-

Two tore through his throat and the other three took his face off. His body hit the ground hard. Blood poured from his neck and face.

***

Yvette hurried to tuck her gun and got out her handcuffs. She cuffed the only remaining man's hands behind his back and looked up, just as Julie walked up, reloading her gun.

"You good?" she asked Julie.

"Yeah. Driver's dead, of course," she said, as the fire spread to other trucks in the row. "Where's the girl at?" she asked.

"I had a security guard take her for me so I could come get yo' crazy ass. Back-up is en route, too."

"Good lookin' out. We need to go check the truck that they were originally in," Julie said, just as they heard the sounds of sirens wailing from close by.

Hauling Caballo up from the ground, she and Yvette headed towards the truck the men had been in. A big group of truck drivers and truck stop staff stood a few hundred feet from where it'd sat. Half of them were looking at the bright ball of fire, created by the burning trucks, some were looking at the truck with bullet holes all in it, with a trailer on bare rims.

Julie took a hairpin from her hair and picked the lock that secured the trailer's swing doors. She got the lock open as a swarm of their squad members infiltrated the lot, accompanied by swarms of Lake County Sheriffs.

The second she opened the doors, and shined her flashlight into the trailer, Julie and Yvette gasped in shock at what they were seeing.

"Oh, my God," Yvette said, as she laid eyes on so many young foreign girls, barely clothed, and all with chains and shackles on as if they were slaves on the Mayflower.

Julie turned to Caballo and hit him hard in his jaw with her gun, shattering it like it was made of glass.

"Creep-ass bitch!" she snapped.

Chapter 11

"You okay, baby?" Yvette asked, as she held Julie with one arm.

After nearly three hours of verbal and written reports, Yvette and Julie had been informed that they had stumbled upon a very tiny piece of a very large scale child sex trafficking ring, run by a dangerous mob of Salvadorians, they had finally made it to their home.

They took showers together, and attempted to eat, but seeing all the young girls chained up like that, then come out of the trailer once they were freed, with marks and bruises all over them, and all of them doped up on heroin, they had no appetite. Out of all forty-two of the kidnapped girls, the oldest one was just fifteen years old.

"No. I am not okay, Yvette," Julie said. "I want to kill every single sick creep bastard that draws breath. Even the ones that haven't committed a criminal sex act yet, should get crushed glass put up their dick holes and have battery acid injected into their veins."

"Wooooow." Yvette released her but gave her a kiss on the top of her head. "I think you'll like the next job that Benicio has for us then. Check it out."

She grabbed the manila file folder and opened it up to the next job. When Julie saw what it was, a sinister smile grew on her face.

"Perfect," she said, ready to get to it already.

***

"Yeees, baby, yeees! Suck that big Black African cock, 'yoo du'ty bitch, 'yoo!" said Melvin, a British adult film production company owner, as he watched the big African man and the ditzy English blonde go crazy for the camera. "Oi' want 'yoo to stuff it *awl* down 'yoor throat! *Awl* of it!"

Behind him, two cameras were filming while the petite British chick that Melvin had brought from England, sucked on nearly eleven inches of Kenyan cock, using two hands to stroke his shaft while she worked her magic on her knees in front of him.

The Kenyan man had remnants of whipped cream, still in his pubic hairs. The rest of it had been licked and slurped off by the girl before she took his dick into her mouth. Leaning against the fridge in the kitchenette of the studio apartment that Melvin had rented for the shoot, the big African's eyes rolled to the back of his head from the phenomenal oral skills the girl had. "Yah! Oh, God! Yas', beetch! Suck 'dis cock good! Suck 'dis muddafucka, baby! Woo! Fuck!" he groaned, grabbing the back of her head so he could face-fuck her.

"Yeeess! Yeeeess! Fuck that cunt's face!" Melvin yelled as he got so turned on that he couldn't resist grabbing his hard dick through his plaid trousers and stroking himself, right next to the two camera men. "Yeeeaaah, baby, yeeaaah! That's great!"

The girl released her partner's cock seconds later and was pulled up from her knees. He pushed her up to the counter, made her face the window and place her hands on the countertop. Getting behind her, he reached for the can of whipped cream that stood by her hand and sprayed it between her ass cheeks.

"Yeeah, baby! Lick it 'awl out of her arse cheeks, 'yoo naughty bloke, 'yoo!" Melvin shouted, jerking his dick harder and faster.

The Kenyan lowered himself down and started licking the whipped cream out of her ass crack. The girl squealed with delight, raising herself up on her tippy toes. She loved it when she had a tongue in her ass. It made her feel so dirty.

Once the Kenyan had licked her clean of the whipped cream, he got up and scooted closer to her. He inserted his hardness into her wetness and started fucking her hard and fast, punishing her.

She moaned out loudly, crying in bliss. She looked back, gritting her teeth, talking shit to him, demanding he fuck her like she was a dirty whore. The Kenyan man grabbed her by her hair with his left hand, and with his right he grabbed her by her throat, choking her while he fucked her.

Melvin saw dollar signs as the African dominated the little white girl. He had a large fan base for his multi-cultural porn flicks, but his biggest fan base was interested in something *waaaaaay* more…illicit.

***

Half an hour later, after the girl took all of the Kenyan's dick in her ass and got a mouthful of cum, the scene wrapped.

"Great joo'b, 'yoo two!" Melvin shouted as he felt wetness in his underwear. "Take 'thurty and we'll meet back here for the coo'nstruction sooi'te scene, yeah?"

The stars and filmers agreed. Melvin hurried out of the little studio and went to the one that was right next to it. He'd made this one a makeshift office. His computer was set up in it, with high-speed internet, and a few cameras for up-close-and-personal shoots that he kept in total secret, were placed around the room.

He went to his desk and pulled out a plastic baggie from the top drawer, filled with a quarter ounce of cocaine. Melvin quickly snorted four big lines off his desk, re-charging himself up. As the cocaine gave him the euphoric bliss that he loved so much, he started wanting to fuck the blonde so badly that his dick began to throb in his trousers. The way she sucked the African man's dick had him dying to stuff his own cock down her throat.

He went to grab his phone and call her over, when knocking at the door stopped him. "What in bloody hell?" he asked himself, covering the mound of cocaine laying on his desk and going to see who was at his door. Peeking out of the peephole, he was surprised to see two women there, wearing the sluttiest cop costumes ever. He immediately unlocked and opened the door.

"Well, hello, thea', ladies? Are you the two new 'guls Oi've been waitin' for?" he asked.

Melvin couldn't help but gaze lustfully at them. They were both in shiny light blue silk cop uniformed tops, black micro-mini pleated skirts, with light blue fishnet pantyhose, and sexy stilettos on their feet.

One was Asian, the other was Black, and they were so amazingly gorgeous that his dick pulsated in his pants at the thought of them "*trying out*" for the position.

"Uh…yes…we're here to please," the Black girl said.

"And we've got toys, to show how we get down," the Asian girl then said, with a grin.

"Oh, goodie! Please! Come in!" Melvin said and stepped aside for them to enter.

Inside, Melvin was filled with glee. He lusted after the two sexy vixens, yearning to sample their goodies for himself before he allowed the world to see them getting fucked and gang banged.

They set their bag down on the bed and stood by it, both of them wearing smiles.

"So," Melvin said, stepping towards them after her locked the door. "What do Oi' 'cawl 'yoo two lovely ladies?"

"Well…" The Black chick pulled out a pair of pink fuzzy handcuffs from behind her back and went towards him. "You can call me, *You Are*," she told him, then she grabbed his wrists and cuffed his hands behind him.

"Oh wow!" Melvin laughed, enjoying the aggressiveness the girl was displaying. "I *love* it! Get wild with me! But, uh, the name? It's a little peculiar to me."

The Asian chick stepped up to him then. "Well then, you should understand perfectly when you hear my name," she told him, as she and her friend walked him over to the bed.

"And they 'cawl 'yoo…what?" Melvin asked, before they threw him on the bed.

"Fucked," the Asian told him, with a demonic smile.

Melvin rolled over onto his stomach and looked at the ladies. "You Are…Fucked?"

They nodded their heads and grinned.

"Oh 'dea," he said, as it began to sink in.

The Asian girl then walked up on him and sent a lightning-fast kick to his jaw, knocking him right out.

***

-SMACK!-

Yvette smacked Melvin awake. He yelped from the sting of her open hand. It took all of five seconds to see that he was ass-naked, tied up by his wrists and ankles to the bed, stretched out like a human starfish.

"Shut up, you perverted-ass bitch!" Julie snapped, then *she* smacked him.

"Ow! What in bloody hell is this?" Melvin demanded to know.

-SMACK!-

Melvin screamed when Yvette smacked him again. "Ooowww! Stop it!"

-SMACK! SMACK! SMACK! SMACK!-

Julie fired his ass up repeatedly. "Did you stop when the little kids you secretly been filming pleaded for you to stop? Huh?" she said to him. "Did you stop those filthy fucking creeps from sticking their dicks inside of them, while you and your *sick-ass* crew made movies of what will pain them for the rest of their goddamn lives?"

Melvin's heart dropped at Julie's words. His eyes went wide in shock. He had been figured out.

"Yeah." Yvette saw the look in his eyes that told him that he knew what was up. "Your career in child pornography is over, creep!"

Julie went and grabbed the bag with her and Yvette's *tools*. She grabbed a small metal cylinder canister with a burner spout. Melvin recognized it as a campfire starter. She grabbed a small plastic bottle of liquid and squirted it all over Melvin's dick.

"No! Wait! Wait! Please!" he begged.

Yvette hurried to go get the ball gag that they had. Julie helped her get it onto the struggling child pornographer, stuffing the ball into his mouth and strapping it in behind his head. His screams and pleas for mercy were now just muffled sounds of bullshit.

Still, Melvin thrashed around, desperate to break free before Julie could do what she was about to do.

"Let's show him how it feels to be helpless and hopeless," Yvette told Julie.

"My pleasure," Julie said, then the ignited the campfire starter.

Melvin tried begging, even with the ball gag in his mouth, but his pleas fell upon deaf ears. Julie put the fire to his dick and lit him up.

The two watched him thrash and yank as his dick and balls burned, melting before their very eyes.

Julie went and poured the lighter fluid on his hands and his feet, and then she lit them up. Yvette went and got a bottle of water and stood by until his hands, feet, and his crotch were nothing but charred stumps.

Melvin whimpered, trembling and shaking in agony. He was in so much pain that he was on the brink of passing out.

Yvette slapped him again, bringing him back. "Fuck, you thought it was over, creep?" she asked.

Julie poured the lighter fluid over his face, which really woke Melvin up.

With the little strength he had left, he tried to beg for his life with the ball in his mouth, but it was useless. Julie lit his face up and together, they watched the child porn movie maker burn to death.

In just over three minutes, he was gone.

"Na na naaa naa na naaa naa…hey hey heeeey…yoooouuuu diiiiiiiiiiiieed," Yvette sang out.

"*Biiiiiiiiiiiiitch*!" Julie added.

Then they both busted out laughing.

***

"Feel better yet?" Yvette asked Julie, as they both watched their costumes, wigs, gloves, and everything they'd taken with them to kill the movie-making creep burn in a fire pit, out at a forest preserve.

"A little. I miss my baby, though," she told Yvette.

Yvette's phone rang just then. She pulled it out of her pocket and rolled her eyes when she saw it was Webster.

"Can I help you?" she answered without even a hint of pleasantness in her voice.

"Sure. Go out to dinner with me tonight," Webster told her, adding a corny-ass chuckle.

"Webster. I did *not* give you my number, which means *you* used departmental resources to find it, and that's *not* protocol. If you call me again. and it has nothin' to do with work, I'ma put some paper on yo' weird ass and you gon' be directin' traffic for the rest of yo' thirsty-ass life. Try me," Yvette dared, then she ended the call.

Julie shook her head. "He makes me wish that Benicio put a hit on *him*."

The sounds of crotch-rocket engines came as Yvette and Julie laughed. They turned and saw T.G. and Bucks coasting their Hayabusas towards them.

Julie gasped. "My baby!" she exclaimed excitedly, taking off and running to Bucks.

Yvette smiled. She went over to where her dude was and threw her arms around his neck, kissing his lips.

"I missed you, baby," she told T.G. as he wrapped his arms around her, hugging her tightly to him.

"Then how about you come with me to Jamaica?" he asked her.

Yvette pulled back and looked at him with surprise. "Jamaica? For real?"

"Yeah. We all could use a vacation. Where better to go for that than a Caribbean paradise that has the greatest food, good drank, *fire-ass* ganja, and some poppin'-ass night clubs?"

"There, but with the two *baddest* bitches in the world," Yvette replied, with big grin.

"For real?" Julie asked Bucks when he suggested what T.G. had to Yvette.

He nodded. "You know they got beaches where muhfuckas can get naked and have a ball 'n shit, right?"

"Uh-uh! Why would I want other people to see *my* man's dick?" Julie asked with a raised eyebrow.

"Because can't no other bitch get it but you," Bucks told her.

She couldn't help but smile at him then. "Hmmmmm. Okay. Jamaica it is."

"Yah 'mon! Off to 'de islands we all go!" Bucks then shouted, geeked that he was going somewhere he had never been in life, with the woman he didn't ever want to be without.

Chapter 12

The following night, the private Lear jet touched down at Kingston's Norman Manley International Airport. Waiting on the tarmac was a blacked-out Mercedes-Benz G55 4x4 Squared, sitting high up on a lift kit with off-road wheels, and equipped with a rammer guard in front.

Posted next to it was a big dark-skinned dread head, with a thick beard, rocking a black tank-top, red Balmain denim shorts with a Louis Vuitton belt, and red Timberlands. The Rolex on his wrist flickered from all the diamonds in it, as did the Cuban link chain around his neck, and the diamond studs in his ears.

The jet taxied up to the G-Wagon and stopped. The stairway descended down, and one by one, the four flyers and the two dogs deplaned, stepping out into the sweltering Caribbean summertime heat.

"Wooooo! *Goddamn,* it's hot as fuck out here!" Yvette exclaimed, hoping that her deodorant would hold up.

T.G. touched the ground behind her and pulled her to him, grinning at her. "You think it's hot out here? Wait 'til we get to where we stayin', bae."

Yvette smiled, licking her lips. "Mmmmmmm…is it gon' be hot and spicy like jerk chicken?"

T.G. planted a kiss on her lips. "Hotter," he told her.

Yvette felt her nipples getting hard at the thought of some spicy Jamaican loving.

When Julie, Bucks, Sir and Rock got off the plane, the big dread head approached with the biggest smile on his face.

"Me niggas! Wha' gwan, wha' gwan!" he shouted, dapping T.G. and Bucks up. "Glad 'ta see 'ya finally made it back hea'."

"Yeah, man," T.G. replied, happy to see the big man and to be back in Kingston. "Been a little too long, but we here now, fam. Yo, check it out. This is my lady, Yvette. Bae, this is me and Bucks's homie. They call him *Chef*."

"Chef?" Yvette and Julie asked curiously.

"Yeah. This nigga be cookin' some *shit*, Joe," chuckled Bucks. "And sometimes, it ain't always food."

Chef laughed. "Nice 'ta meet 'ya, Yvette."

She smiled and shook his hand. "Likewise, Chef."

"Chef, this is my lady, Julie," Bucks said. "We all call her JuJu, though."

Chef nodded and shook Julie's hand.

"Okay, 'den. Me bwoi Bucks got himself a China mama, eh?" he said.

"I'm Vietnamese," Julie corrected.

"Bomba-clot, 'mon! Me 'ear a *lot* a 'bout 'de women of Vietnam! 'Ya play no games when it comes to 'de rough life!"

T.G., Yvette, and Bucks all laughed as Julie struck a strong girl pose, representing her people's strength, as they were known to have.

After he was told the dogs' names, Chef was ready to get back into his G-Wagon and head to his neck of the woods. They all got their luggage off the jet, loaded the Mercedes truck up and hopped in.

"Me glad 'ya all came 'tru, T.G.," Chef said as he pulled off, grabbing the spliff he had in the center cup holder. "But ya need to be cautious, we been warrin' wit' 'de bomba-clot AK Boyz, and 'de Constabulary muddafuckas really hard lately. 'Ya no go nowhere 'wit out a gun, 'ya 'ear me, rude bwoi?"

T.G. nodded his head. "Noted."

Chef handed the spliff to T.G. and told him to spark it up. T.G. lit it and off the first puff, nearly hacked up a lung from how ridiculously strong it was.

"Damn! Fuck is this?" he asked Chef, with bloodshot red eyes.

"Dat 'dere is *real* green, me nigga! Man 'dat shit up, nigga! Man it up, I tell 'ya!"

Yvette, Julie, and Bucks, all in the back, were laughing their asses off, until they got the spliff in *their* hands, and the smoke in *their* lungs.

Chef laughed his ass off at them, all high as kites before he made it ten minutes away from the airport. They were stuck, staring out the windows, not knowing if they were coming or going. As the spliff made it back to him, he put it between his lips and puffed, while he reached to the dashboard and turned the music up, blasting an old Beanie Man song.

***

From the airport, Chef drove to what was called Tivoli Gardens, where he was born and raised. It was the slums. Worse than what many found in America. There, there were no rules or laws. It was kill or be killed if you were in the streets. Gangsters against cops, and gangsters against gangsters.

Turning down a street lined with brick buildings on both sides, Yvette and Julie looked around, taking it all in. It took them back to when they watched all the gangster movies that had been filmed in, or had parts filmed in Kingston.

Colorful structures never let you forget that you were in the Caribbean, but broken-down cars, dilapidated houses, and crazy looking front yards never let you forget, that you were in the hood…for real.

Chef pulled up to a building with a big window. Through it, Yvette and Julie could see people enjoying food and drinks inside. Above it, they saw a sign that said, *"Momma's House."*

"Me know 'ya all got 'de munchies from 'de ganja. Momma gots food ready for 'ya. Come. Let's go inside," Chef said.

"What about the dogs?" Yvette asked, rubbing behind Sir's ears.

"Bring 'em. Momma *loves* dogs," T.G. told her.

They got out of the G-Wagon, hit with the heat again until they got inside of the air-conditioned restaurant. Inside, the aromas of so many different meals had their mouths watering. The dogs' sense of smell went haywire from such delicious aromas.

Every single person inside, all shouted out to Chef like he was a celebrity when they entered. A table with beautiful women all hollered to him, blowing him kisses, giving him googly eyes.

"Tremaine! Bernard!"

Yvette and Julie heard the sound of a woman's voice. They turned and saw a tall buxom ebony-toned woman with long gray dreads, wearing a flower-print dress, sandals, and an apron walking their way with a huge smile on her face.

"Me nephews have returned 'ta see Big Momma!" she shouted.

T.G. and Bucks emphatically hugged the large woman when she got to them. Yvette and Julie smiled at the picture. She could tell that their men and the two dread heads were very close.

Looking a little harder, they could see the similarities in Chef's face and the woman's. They surmised that they had to be mother and son.

When the lady released T.G. and Bucks, Chef made the introductions.

"Momma, 'dis is Yvette, T.G.'s woman, 'de 'otha 'gal is JuJu, Bernard's lady."

Momma was ecstatic to meet them. She gave them both huge hugs, welcoming them like they were family. When she turned her attention to the dogs, she went bananas with excitement. Sir and Rock both got hyped up when she gave them belly rubs. Yvette and Julie knew their dogs well and saw that the two German Shepherds had instantaneously created a bond with the woman.

"Me hope 'ya all are hungry. Here at Momma's House, any'ting 'ya want, I can make. What will 'ya have?" she asked them.

Decisions were made. The girls picked jerk chicken, T.G. got the curry goat, Bucks picked sancocho, a stew made with seven different meats, rice, and vegetables. Chef went to assist his mother in cooking for them.

While they waited, sodas and a plate of oxtails were brought out for them and the dogs. They dined on the delicious morsels, then dove into their food when their plates came. With their munchies gone, stomachs full, the girls and their men left big tips on the table for Momma.

Hopping back into Chef's G-Wagon, they bent the corner and continued riding through Chef's *Garrison*, arriving in a section with recently renovated two-story houses lining both sides of the street.

People were outside, smoking weed on their porches and posted along the street. Some had pistols tucked into their waistlines, with AK-47s close by. Kids rode around on bikes and / or played in blow-up pools.

Yvette and Julie were super excited to be there. They were in a place where the realest gangsters on earth came from.

"Me must remind 'ya all. Keep 'dem eyes open for 'de pussy-hole AK Boyz, and 'de bomba-clot Constabularies. Pussy muddafuckas ride 'tru 'hea like 'dis is 'dier garrison. We gonna teach 'dem muddafuckas that Tivoli Gardens belongs to 'de Shower Posse!" Chef told them.

"Shower Posse?" Yvette questioned.

T.G. told her about the infamous mob from Tivoli Gardens. They were *not* people anybody wanted to have on their bumpers.

Chef pulled up to a decent-looking two-story house and parked at the curb. As they all got out of his G-Wagon, many people that were out and about shouted out to Chef, saluting him.

Chef led them into the house and showed them around. It was fixed up, cozy and vibrant with colors. The bedrooms were luxurious, all with glass sliding doors that opened up to elevated decks. The backyard had a fence surrounding it, perfect for Sir and Rock to run around in.

He then took them down to where the single-car garage was behind the house. Inside, a 2012 Mercedes-Benz S600, sporting champagne-colored paint, with twenty-one-inch chromed AMG rims, and dark tinted windows. Chef gave T.G. the key to it, then lastly, he took them to a secret room that was built in behind a small utility room. The wall inside was fitted with racks of revolvers, semi-automatic handguns, assault rifles, and boxes of ammunition stacks up. There were even bulletproof vests hanging up.

"This is a room for someone that sees war bein' an imminent thing," Bucks said, amazed by the arsenal of weapons.

"War is *always* imminent, bae," Julie told him. "Trust and believe in that."

"We no play games out hea' in our neck of 'de woods," Chef told them all. "Ya no go nowhea' 'wit out a 'gat, 'ya 'ear me?"

"We don't play no games out *our* neck of the woods either, Chef," Yvette told him.

"None at all," Julie added.

Chef nodded his head. He dapped T.G. and Bucks, then gave the ladies hugs, then he left them all to get settled in.

Yvette and Julie took the dogs and let them out into the backyard, setting up food and water bowls for them.

"*Soooo...*" Yvette took her dude's hand and smiled up at him while sliding his hand up her skirt so he could feel her wetness, since she wasn't wearing any panties. "What's up with that hot 'n spicy stuff you's talkin' about, *rude bwoi*?" she asked him.

T.G scooped her up off her feet. "Wasn't nothin' about talkin', lil mama," he told her, then without wasting another minute, he whisked her off to their bedroom to handle make good on what he had told her earlier.

Still in the big living room, Julie pushed Bucks down onto the long leather couch, and jumped on him, straddling his lap. She kissed him wildly as his hands raised her skirt up, palming her ass. She was hot and ready for some him, and he was ready for some her.

They lip boxed with each other. Julie's temperature rose sky high as if she was outside of the a/c-cooled home, out in the hot Jamaican sun. Bucks stood up with her still on his lap. He set her on her feet and stripped her out of her shirt, bra, pulled her thong down, making her keep her skirt and her stilettos on.

Julie relieved him of all his clothes, then she dropped down to her knees before him, taking him into her mouth. Bucks cursed when she deep throated him. She took all of him to the back of her throat, making herself gag. He put his hand on the back of her head and fucked her mouth like it was a pussy. His eyes rolled to the back of his head from how bomb her warm wet mouth felt.

"Shit! Goddamn this shit feel so muthafuckin' good!" he groaned.

Julie added two hands and started twist-stroking his shaft while she sucked. Bucks's toes curled up so hard that he thought they'd break off. He groaned and cursed while she pleased him. When he couldn't take it anymore, he took his cock away from her, tossed her onto the couch and dropped to his knees in front of *her*, to please her.

"Oooooo, shhh-shhhiiiiit! Buuuuucks!" she moaned out, as he slurped and sucked on her clit.

He held her legs open wide, dining on her like she was the sancocho he had just devoured. He loved how she tasted, and he loved how she moaned his name. He loved pleasing his chick. She was his queen. There wasn't anything he wouldn't do to give her the ultimate "O."

***

Over in their bedroom, Yvette was on all fours, face-down ass up, with ten inches of T.G. inside of her. All she had on was her leather miniskirt and her spike-toed Red Bottoms. With the deck doors open, a fresh Caribbean breeze blowing in, and reggae music crooning through the audio system that was in the bedroom, T.G. pounded Yvette hard and fast from the back. He pulled her hair, smacked on her phat juicy ass and made her scream out his name repeatedly, as if he was trying to make the neighbors learn his name.

"Ooohhh, God! T.G.! I love you! Oh, fuck, I love you, baby!" Yvette cried out as she came close to climaxing.

T.G. grunted and cursed. "Fuck! I love yo' ass, too, bae! And this juicy-ass pussy! I love both of y'all!"

Then he pulled his dick out of her pussy. Yvette reached back and gripped her ass cheeks, opening them up for him. He put the tip to her puckered asshole and eased in, ready to get *all* the way nasty.

***

Bucks's eyes rolled to the back of his head. He groaned, toes curling up. Julie's warm mouth swallowing his dick had him so close to busting another nut. She worked him so good, sucking him, jerking him, deep throating all of him.

100

Julie loved to please her man. The sounds he made when she gave him head made her pussy drip like a broken faucet.

A minute later, Bucks grunted, eyes rolling to the back of his head like he was possessed. He came hard seconds after. Julie milked him for it all, letting her mouth fill up with hot globby cum. She spit his nut back out onto his dick, then she slurped it back up, swallowing it like it was the most delicious treat ever.

"Goddamn, girl. I don't know what I did to get a freak like you, but I'm glad I do have you," he told her.

"Aww!" Julie got up and climbed onto his lap. She wrapped her arms around his neck and stared down into his eyes. "Tell me you love me, Bernard."

"I love you, JuJu. You know that, though."

"I do." She leaned down and kissed his lips. "I love you, too, baby. You gon' be my husband one day, then you gonna give me some babies to take care of while you bringin' in the bacon."

"Black and Vietnamese babies...I have never seen that before." Bucks chuckled.

Julie smiled. "I'm sure there's some in the world somewhere, but it don't matter, our babies are gonna be the *shit*. More than the Kardashian babies."

Bucks was loving the sound of pro-creating with Julie and making her his wife. She was down to ride, beautiful as hell, and was getting money. There was no better woman on earth than the sexy Asian gangstress that was naked on his lap.

His dick got hard again. Julie felt it and smiled as her pussy started getting wet again.

"Oh yeah," he told her. "We still got plenty of fuckin' to do before we leave up outta here."

"Sheeeit, you ain't said nothin' but a word, handsome," she told him. Then she lifted up a little, grabbed his cock and slid her wetness over it, so she could ride him like she was in the rodeo.

***

Yvette squealed, clenching the blanket in her hands, gritting her teeth while T.G. fucked her ass with one knee up. "Fu-fu-fuuuuuuuck, baby! Ooooo, it feels so goooooood!" she cried out, burying her face in the blanket.

"Yeeaah, baby! Tell daddy again how much you like it when I put this dick in that phat ass!" T.G. commanded of her.

"Yes! Baby, I love—"

-BRRRRRRRRRRRRRRRRBRRRRRRRRRRRRR!
-BRRRRRRRRRRRBRRRRRRRRRRRRRRRR!
-BRRRRRRRRRRRRBRRRRRRRRRRRR!-

-BOC! BOC! BOC! BOC! BOC! BOC! BOC! BOC! BOC! BOC!-

-BOOM! BOOM! BOOM! BOOM! BOOM! BOOM! BOOM! BOOM! BOOM!-

Gunshots filled the air like loud strikes of thunder from right outside the house. T.G immediately reacted, grabbing Yvette and rolling off the bed, taking her to the floor and covering her body with his own.

The shots continued for nearly five long minutes before they heard engines revving and tires screeching. They could hear men shouting and yelling seconds later.

"You okay?" T.G. asked her, still covering her.

"No! What the fuck, man? I was about to nut!" Yvette growled angrily.

"Yvette! T.G.!"

Just then, they heard Julie's voice outside their door. From outside, they could also hear Sir and Rock barking from the backyard.

T.G. hopped up and hurried to put his boxers on. He threw Yvette his shirt for her to put on.

"Yo! Bro! Yvette!" yelled Bucks, beating on the door.

T.G. ran to the door and opened it. Julie flew in, wearing a fluffy robe, running right to Yvette, relieved to see that she was unharmed. Bucks stepped in, feeling his heart still pounding in his chest. The gunshots were so close, and since they hadn't flown into his and Julie's room, he had automatically assumed that they might have hit up his homie and Yvette's room.

Seeing they were all good, filled Bucks and Julie with relief. They went out to the balcony that was at the front of the house. Cursing and heated arguments amongst a few men in a huge group of Shower Posse goons, all of them with weapons, got their attention. They then saw Chef approach, holding an AK. Everyone got quiet when he stepped up and spoke.

"'De bomba-clot AK Boyz must die! All of 'dem! Right now!" he shouted.

The mob all held their weapons up and shouted, cheering on their leader's decree.

"Death to 'de opps! Death to 'de opps!" they started chanting.

They all then ran to their whips, hopped in, and sped off, following each other like a *Mad Max* motorcade.

"I'm guessin' that it's about to go down. Sooooo, can we, um… like, ya know… finish what we were doin', before we end up havin' to get on some gangsta shit 'round here, baby?" Yvette asked, *still* so horny.

"Sounds like a good idea to me, love," T.G. said.

He took her from the balcony, back to their room and took her down, while Bucks got back to it with his woman, in the living room again.

Chapter 13

Five Days Later...

Yvette, Julie, T.G, and Bucks had been having a ball for the last few days. Kingston had proven to be the most eventful place they had ever been. They went exploring the old towns of the island, went ATV riding, snorkeling, and rum tasting. Then shooting out to Negril, they got to experience the *adult-only* beaches, enjoying some fun in the sun with no clothes on.

Every night, they either went out to eat, or to a club. They smoked ganja, sipped Jamaican rum. Sir and Rock got to join in on the fun when Chef directed T.G. and Bucks to take the ladies and their dogs to where they could hunt live animals. Two wild pigs were set loose for the German Shepherds.

Yvette and Julie were able to watch their dogs on cameras set up around the area designated for the hunting grounds, catch the pigs and tear them up. It was as exciting as watching a Great White shark catch a seal and rip it to pieces.

***

Chef told them about the Shower Posse's block party for the Gardens early Saturday morning. He told them that there were big reggae stars coming to perform, and big dogs from all over Kingston would be there, along with the most beautiful women that Jamaica had.

Yvette and Julie were thrilled to be going to a real hood block party. They were visualizing it to look like a Sean Paul music video and what they saw on *Belly*, when DMX went to Jamaica to handle Sosa for Ox. For the occasion, they got out their sexiest, most enticing outfits that were dazzling enough to make *every* dick hard, and every pussy wet.

***

"Gooooooddaaamn! I'm fuckin' fried, Joe!" T.G. could barely move on the couch from how zooted he was.

Sir was laid out next to him, relaxing after Yvette had given him a bath.

Hearing Yvette laugh from the bedroom, then the sounds of her high heels clacking on the hardwood floor, he somehow managed to turn his head and look at the entryway.

"That's what cho' ass gets for thinkin' you could puff that ganja shit like that whack-ass loud you smoke on back home, bae," she told him.

T.G. heard her, but he paid no attention to her words. His eyes were on her and the unbelievably sexy, blue sheer, see-through lace mini dress she had on. If it wasn't for the blue bra and the blue thong she had on, she might as well have just called it Saranwrap.

Her hair was done up like she was definitely planning on attracting some attention. Her makeup up was perfect, and her legs were freshly waxed and oiled up. On her feet, she had on shiny blue pointed-toe stiletto pumps.

She looked mighty delicious. So good that T.G. felt his dick hardening up to the point that it started throbbing in his Balmains.

"Wow…I would get up right now and come kiss you while I rub on that phat ass booty…but I'm so high I might fall if I try."

Yvette busted out laughing. She then turned around, about-facing, so he could see how the back of her tiny thong was swallowed up in the crack of her ass. T.G's eyes went even wider, dick pulsating like it was an EMP device, when she bent all the way over, grabbing her ankles and started making it clap.

"Maaaaaan…yo' ass getting' pregnant tonight," he told her, as he watched her meaty butt cheeks clap.

Yvette started laughing her ass off again, while she continued getting her Megan Thee Stallion on.

***

Bucks motor boated Julie's breasts, unable to resist when she emerged from the bedroom, wearing a burnt-orange long-sleeved mini-dress that was completely see-through like Yvette's. The stilettos on her feet matched and had gold spikes in the toes. Her hair was moussed and styled to look wet, and her makeup was minimal, but still emphasized her natural beauty.

Julie giggled from how Bucks's lips felt against her chest. The affection he always showed her kept a big smile on her face. She loved how he was always over her, which kept her pussy wet and yearning for him.

"Baaaeeee," she playfully whined, when he stopped vibrating her bosom, and wrapped his arms around her, pulling him to her. "Come ooooon, we gotta go meet Yvette and T.G. We can't do that if you make me strip you naked and get to fuckin' yo' brains out again."

"Then let's stay in and fuck all night," Bucks suggested, kissing and licking on her neck, heating her up to the point that she was feeling like she could spontaneously combust.

"Buuuuck!" She pulled back, pumping his brakes. "Look, you horny motherfucker. Stop bein' so damn horny and march your ass to the door, goddammit!"

Bucks jumped to attention and raised his hand to his forehead. "Ma'am, yes, ma'am!" he told her, then dipped in and stole one more kiss, before he marched to the door.

Julie smiled so hard as she watched him go, thinking, *God, I freakin' love him so much!*

She went and grabbed her handbag and followed her man out of their room, ready to go turn up Shower Posse style.

***

The streets were blocked off and filled with so many people, young and old. Reggae music blasted from a live DJ stand, where a make-shift stage was built under a pavilion in the middle of a big four-way crossing.

Yvette and Julie saw a ridiculously thick and gorgeous ebony-skinned woman on stage that went by the name *Spice*, performing a song called "Size Matters." Large groups of women were in the middle of the street, twerking and pussy popping for all the fellas that were watching with lust-filled eyes.

Weed smoke filled the air, creating such a thick haze that whoever *wasn't* smoking, *still* got high.

Spice then welcomed Sean Paul and Shaggy on stage with her. They started turning the crowd up even more when they got to performing their song, "Go Down Deh."

In front of their dudes, Yvette and Julie danced enticingly, grinding up against T.G.'s and Bucks's crotches that it was a wonder that neither of the two caught on fire.

T.G. and Bucks gripped and squeezed booty cheeks while wet pussy grinded on their bone-hard dicks. All four of them were high as hell, tipsy from some super strong Jamaican rum. They were in the mood to get naked in front of everyone and fuck each other's brains out like they did on the naked beach in Negril.

Two more artists took the stage, announcing themselves as Kafu Banton and Jorkan. They started rapping their song "Jamaica," and to Yvette and Julie's surprise, when they listened to the two men rap, they realized that the two were rapping in Spanish.

"This is the Caribbean, baby," T.G. told Yvette, as he held onto her hips, moving her body with his to the beat. "Jamaicans, Dominicans, Puerto Ricans, they all run this part of the world. All of the cultures that were created by the strongest and bravest slaves that got off of the slave ships back then when them punk-ass crackers came and took them, mixed together and became prevalent in the tropics."

Yvette's heart fluttered in her chest. She wrapped her arms around his neck, pulled him down and kissed his lips. "Fine as hell, a straight goon, a boss, *and* educated. Tremaine, you are a dream come true."

"And you are the epitome of *Black perfection*, baby," T.G. replied to her. "You and I are a team. It takes two to make the motto, '*Team work makes the dream work*' a true statement. You and I, Yvette, we can do some *real* big things together, baby."

"Yes, we can, and yes we will, T.G.," Yvette said, then she got her another sweet kiss on the lips.

Suddenly, the sounds of screaming trumped the music. Gunshots rang out from somewhere. The music abruptly stopped, and the artists were quickly ushered off the stage by their security.

-BRRRRRRRRRRBRRRRRRRR!-
-BRRRRRRRR! BRRRRRRRR!-
-BOCKA! BOCKA! BOCKA! BOCKA! BOCKA!-
-BRRRRRRRRRRRRRRRRRRRRRRRRRRRRRRRRRRRRRR!-

Assault rifles and pistols popped. Innocent bystanders dropped. The humongous crowd of people scattered like a school of fish when a Great White comes along to eat.

They all ducked low out of instinct, unsure of where the shots were coming from. A second later, blood suddenly splashed on Yvette's face. A young girl that had been next to her was hit by a stray bullet, right in her head.

Pandemonium filled the streets as all hell had broken loose. T.G. and Bucks knew they had to get their ladies up out of there. They hurried them through the panicking crowd, keeping them close to their own bodies.

They heard Chef's unmistakable voice just then. Yvette and Julie saw him and his mob with their choppers running towards where everyone was running from.

Bucks then shouted out at the top of his lungs as pain exploded in his right upper back and in his right thigh. Julie screamed when she realized that he had just been shot.

"Bernard! Baby!" she cried as he fell to the ground in agony.

"Bro!" T.G. immediately dropped down to get his home boy up. "Bae!" he yelled to Yvette, handing her his gun. "Take JuJu's hand! I got bro! Come on!"

He lifted Bucks up, looping his left arm over his shoulder, then soldiered along with him behind the girls. Bucks cursed from the severe stinging, but manned it up, knowing that death was a sure thing if he stopped. They cut to their right, breaking off from the crowds, running through a gangway between two houses. They entered a backyard and came to a tall wooden fence. T.G. set his guy next to the fence and took Yvette's hand, helping her up and over, then he helped Julie over. He was about to help Bucks over, when gunshots came right in their direction, hitting the ground, inches away at their feet.

"Stop! Constabulary! Freeze or die!" they heard a man yell.

T.G. and Bucks looked and saw a big group of men, in tactical SWAT-like gear, with AR-15s and riot helmets.

"Run!" T.G. hurriedly yelled to Yvette and Julie, right before the cops surrounded them.

***

"Shit!" Julie whispered as she looked through a little hole in the fence, seeing her and Yvette's men get cornered.

"Shit, *nothing*!" Yvette shot back. "You sound like that's all she wrote or somethin'!"

"How the fuck is we gon' get 'em back, Yvette? Them cops are deep as fuck!"

Yvette pulled out her phone, glad to see that she still got signal. As fast as she could, she sent an emergency text to the one person that made it a point to let them know to call him if they needed him.

"Okay. Come on," she then told Julie, then she took off running along the fence, leading Yvette on, looking for where the fence ended, or wherever they could get over it.

***

"Oh, you two are American, eh?" the big-nosed chief of the Constabulary cops asked, looking at T.G.'s and Bucks's driver's licenses that he had two of the twelve men he had with him search the two for, and along with finding their wallets, the cops had found the Glocks that T.G. and Bucks had tucked in their waistlines. "Carryin' illegal guns in *my* garrison, runnin' from me, *and* 'ya not even from 'hea? You two are fucked! 'Ya know 'dat, right? Take 'dem!" he demanded his men.

T.G. was cuffed, and ignoring the two gunshot wounds that Bucks had been bleeding from, they cuffed him as well. The two were nearly dragged from the backyard, out to the street where an Isuzu pick-up truck with seats in the bed idled at the curb, with two SUVs and more men posted around it.

"Hey! Hold up!"

The chief heard a woman hollering. Looking up the street, he saw two ladies in tight dresses and heels, running towards them.

T.G. and Bucks saw them and cursed under their breath, wondering to themselves, why in the hell did the girls not run?

"Freeze!" the chief shouted, as his men all pointed their assault rifles at them. "Stop, or you will be shot!"

"No! Don't shoot! We're American cops!" he heard one of the women shout. "We're State Police from Illinois! We're here to extradite those two back to Illinois to face drug-trafficking charges!"

The Chief gestured for his men to lower their weapons.

What the hell are they up to? Posin' as cops? T.G. wondered to himself.

"Show me identification, and your badges!" yelled the chief. "If you are lying 'ta me, you will die right 'hea!"

What the fuck are y'all doin'? Get outta here! thought Bucks, as he continued to lose blood.

The chief pulled out his semi-automatic pistol and waited as the two women approached. In the light that shone over where he and his men stood, he got a better look at the girls. He immediately had wild thoughts fill his head, looking at how scantily clad they were.

The two pulled out their wallets, which had their badges in them. The chief looked at them without touching them, then he looked at the women, with a sadistic smile. "Come!" he barked. "You will come to me station and be verified!" He took it upon himself to search the ladies after ordering his men to watch his back. He tucked his gun and took their purses, which had their guns in them. Despite the fact that they were wearing tiny see-through dresses, he patted them down from their ankles to their chests, then he rubbed both of their asses, squeezing each cheek.

Sitting up in the Constabulary's pick-up truck, T.G. and Bucks were seeing red as they practically watched the pig hand-molest their ladies.

"Okay. Up 'ya go," said the Chief.

He again was the one to "help" the ladies. He pushed them up by their asses onto the back of the Isuzu. The rest climbed up, while the others got into the other vehicles, then they all sped off to get back to the station.

Passing a few houses, Yvette saw him step out of the shadows, looking at them being carted off. He slid back into the shadows a second later, disappearing from her sight.

Okay, rude bwoi.......don't let us down......please, she thought.

Feeling eyes on her, Yvette turned her head back and saw one of the constabulary guys staring at her. He licked his lips and smiled, revealing a dingy gold-toothed smile.

Yvette nearly threw up in her mouth.

Chapter 14

The driver behind the wheel of the pick-up backed it up into the station's rear garage entry point and killed the engine. The other SUVs backed in with it, then the door was shut and secured.

"This man needs medical attention, Chief!" Julie demanded, seeing how much blood had leaked from Bucks onto the floorboard of the pick-up, now that they were in a brightly lit garage. "Why have you not taken him to a hospital?"

"No 'doctas on call at 'dis time of night. Him just got a flesh wound. Him no die," the man told her, with a shit-eating grin. "Please. Come inside and relax. I will verify 'ya, and if 'ya two are who 'ya say 'ya are, then 'ya can go."

"With *them*, right?" Yvette asked, as she stepped down from the pick-up.

The chief smiled at her. "Sure."

He led them, his men, and the two captives into the station through a doorway. Inside, it looked like a dungeon. T.G. and Bucks were put inside of an iron cage and locked inside. The other constabularies went into a small breakroom, leaving the ladies to follow the chief.

He took them to his office, stepped aside as they entered, then he shut and locked the door behind him. Walking around his cluttered desk, he sat in his high-backed cotton chair, putting his dirty combat-style boots up on the desk.

113

"So... 'Ya been enjoyin' Jamaica so far?" he asked them. "Go to any of 'de naked beaches?"

"Yes," Yvette told him as she and Julie stood side by side in front of his desk, arms folded, scowling at him. "Never experienced anything like it."

"Aren't you supposed to be verifyin' who we are?" Julie snapped, beyond ready to drive a sharp pencil through the man's eyehole.

"Julie... be nice, girl," Yvette said to her, giving her a look when Julie shot her a look. "I think the chief is interested in tellin' us about the experiences we could have here."

"'Dat is correct," the chief spoke. "Lots of experiences to be had 'hea in Jamaica, good Caribbean food, good rum, and...good love."

"Ooooo! I haven't gotten to experience anything even remotely close to good love since we've been here, sir," Yvette told him. "It kind of sounds like, you might know a thing or two about that, Big Chief."

Julie watched her lover and friend inch her way around the desk, until she was right at the chief's side, so close that the man could probably feel her body heat.

The chief took his feet off the desk and turned himself to face her. Smiling, he looked up at the beautiful woman. "Me know *all* about love, beautiful 'gal," he told her.

Yvette sat herself up on his desk then, over-lapping her right leg over her left, letting him see her mouth-wateringly sexy thigh. The chief licked his lips as he envisioned licking her up and down until she said stop. "I would *love* to learn, handsome." She then uncrossed her leg, turned and positioned herself so that she faced him with her legs open.

The chief turned to her, looking down. He could see right up her see-through dress. His dick grew bone hard at the sight of the tiny strip of fabric that concealed her goodie box. "'Ya wan' learn 'de language of love, eh? Me can show 'ya what 'ya wanna' know, baby. Me eat pussy good like Rottweiler eat robber. Me got 'de skills of a porn star."

Yvette smiled at him, moaning, licking her lips. She opened her legs all the way for him. "Talk is cheap, *Chief.* How about you let yo' lips and tongue *prove* it?"

He slid forward and leaned his face down between her legs. He smelled her and moaned from how good her womanhood smelled.

Julie watched in disgust as he kissed the insides of Yvette's thighs, then licked up to her thong.

Balancing on her hands, Yvette leaned back and let him pull her thong off with his teeth. He pulled it down her legs and tossed it, then he stuck his face all the way between her thick thighs and ran his tongue up her slit, tasting her honey.

"Mmmmm. Tastes so good, little mama. I get wild now," he told her, then went to dive in to go crazy.

-*CLICK CLACK*-

The chief froze when he heard the sound that he knew all too well. He felt the barrel of cold steel touch the back of his head.

"Pull yo' muthafuckin' face from between *my* bitch's legs, or the only thing you gon' eat tonight is lead!" Julie told him.

Yvette removed herself from his desk as the chief put his hands up. The look on his face made her laugh her ass off.

"Pussy gets 'em *every* time," she said, shaking her head. "Thirsty-ass niggas always think because they can eat some pussy, that a bitch like me gon' fall for a clown?"

-*CRACK!*-

Yvette cocked back and rocked the chief in his jaw.

Julie then bashed him in the back of the head with his own gun, knocking him out cold.

The door flew open just then. Julie pointed the Glock towards the doorway, ready to pop, but relaxed when she saw Chef there, dressed in all-black with a black bandana tied around his neck, and two MAC-11s with fifty-round clips and silencers in his hands.

"Whoa, whoa! It's me, JuJu! Relax!" Chef told her.

"Where's Bucks and T.G.?" she pleaded to know, as Yvette got the chief's cuffs out from his utility belt and cuffed his hands behind his back.

"They are safe. Me bruddas got 'dem and smoked the other constabulary bomba-clots. 'Dey are both en route to Momma's right now."

Julie sighed in relief that her and Yvette's men were safe and already out of there.

"How did you get past the others?" Yvette wanted to know.

Chef looked at her and grinned. "'De Shower Posse does no sneakin' around, we go right in and kill *everybody* without makin' a sound."

He walked over to where the chief lay, just as the crooked leader started to wake up from his temporary nap. When he opened his eyes, he saw two machine guns pointing at his face.

"Me knew me shoulda' made 'ya whore momma abort 'ya," he said to Chef. "A disgrace, 'ya are! A disgrace!"

Yvette and Julie gasped as they realized what was being said.

"Me a *man*, bitch-ass nigga!" Chef snapped between clenched teeth. "Me more a man 'den you will eva' be! 'Ya neva' be worthy for me 'ta refer 'ta 'ya as me father! Rot in hell, pussy!"

The chief shouted as Chef squeezed both triggers.

-PFFFFFFFFFFFFFFFFFFFFFFFFFFFFFFFFFFFT!-
-PFFFFFFFFFFFFFFFFFFFFFFFFFFFFFFFFFFFT!-

Chef blasted his biological father until both of his guns clicked empty. The chief had rocked and flopped as .45 caliber rounds repeatedly entered his body. After a hundred rounds wet him up, Chef looked down at the barely recognizable man that had impregnated his mother, twenty-five years ago.

"Bitch," Chef spat, with the barrels of his guns smoking hot.

Yvette and Julie stayed silent as Chef took a minute to get himself together.

When he was done, he looked at them. "Let's go. Your men are wating for 'ya two," he said to them. "Go out. Me bruddas are out 'dea waiting. I'll clean up 'dis mess."

"Are you okay, Chef?" Yvette asked, as the strong realization of him having just killed his father hit her.

Chef nodded his head. "Me a real rude bwoi, I kill for fun. I kill for my family and me bruddas. Me have no heart for 'de bomba-clot fuckery. 'Ya go on now. I be right out, 'ya ear me?"

Yvette nodded, then she and Julie hurried out of the station, right to where a mob of Shower Posse goons awaited with big guns, posted up where an Escalade ESV sat with Chef's Mercedes truck. Less than five minutes later, they saw Chef walk out of the building. He got halfway to them when it exploded, sending a massive fireball up into the pitch-black sky. He didn't even blink from the loud and powerful blast.

The ladies hopped up into the G-Wagon with the Shower Posse leader. Chef slammed it into drive and mashed the gas, dipping off with them safely rescued from what could've been a very bad situation, as the building and the bodies they left inside of it, burned to ashes.

***

Julie and Yvette ran right to Bucks and T.G. when they saw them sitting on a couch inside of Momma's house. Bucks had been sewed up and patched up. T.G sat across from his homie. The girls were overjoyed that the two were safe.

They hugged their men, but to their surprise, neither T.G., nor Bucks hugged them back. They barely acknowledged them.

Staying quiet, Chef and Momma already knew what was up. They left out of the room, leaving the four alone, not wanting to see any more fireworks.

"Hey! Baby, what's wrong?" Julie asked Bucks when he moved his head as she went to kiss him on his lips.

Yvette got the same spin-move from T.G.

"T.G.? What the hell is yo' problem? I know you ain't mad at us for stickin' around?" she asked, putting her hands on her hips.

Bucks gave no reply, nor eye contact. T.G stood and moved away from Yvette, walking towards a window. The girls both glanced at each other, staying where they were.

"Hello! Tremaine!" shouted Yvette.

"Bernard!" yelled Julie.

"Y'all played us," T.G. finally spoke, turning to face them. "You two are cops...for *real!*"

Yvette and Julie both felt their hearts drop. Bucks still remained silent. He was hot with fury for being led on for so long. He'd fallen in love with a chick that he now realized, he didn't know from a can of paint.

"Okay! Yes...we're Illinois State troopers, in the narcotics division, Tremaine! But, what's wrong with that?" Yvette asked, standing up from where she sat.

"Y'all been gatherin' info on us to get us knocked," Bucks said, finally speaking, though still refusing to look at Julie.

She shot up then and gave him an incredulous look. "Bucks! How the fuck could you say some dumb shit like that?" she demanded to know, marching right up to him with fire in her eyes.

He glared at her. "Back up. I am *not* playin' with you, JuJu."

"I ain't movin' nowhere 'til you remember who *I* am to *you*! That I love you, and that you love me!"

He laughed at her and waved her off. "Fuck outta here, Joe. Back up off me, shorty, before I slap the fuck out cho' ass."

"Hey! Bernard! Watch yo' muthafuckin' mouth! Don't you ever threaten my girl again, nigga!" Yvette screamed, walking towards him with her fists balled up.

"Yvette! Chill the fuck out!" T.G. yelled out.

"No!" she shot back at him. "Fuck all that shit! How in the actual fuck can y'all really be pissed that we kept *our* jobs to ourselves?"

"What would you two have said if we told y'all?" Julie threw in, as tears filled her eyes. "Or thought?"

"The same shit we're sayin' now, shortie!" Bucks snapped at her. "Fuck the po-lice!"

"Let's ride, bruh, before we really end up cuffed and in a cage, somewhere in eastkabumfuck," said T.G. "Have a nice life, *Officers*."

"Tremaine!" Yvette went after T.G. as he and Bucks rushed away from them.

Stuck and speechless, feeling like her heart had been cut out of her chest with a rusty knife and stepped on, Julie stood there, with tears rolling down her face, as she watched the only man that she had ever loved, leave her in pieces.

The door slammed in Yvette's face before she could grab T.G. She stepped back, looked at it with shock, then she burst into tears, crying her eyes out, sinking down to the floor as Julie wailed out of control.

Chapter 15

Three Weeks Later...

-BOC! BOC! BOC! BOC! BOC! BOC! BOC! BOC!-
-BOOM! BOOM! BOOM! BOOM! BOOM! BOOM!-
-BRRRRRRRRR! BRRRRRRRRR!
-BRRRRRR! BRRRRRRRRR!-
-POW! POW! POW! POW! POW! POW!-

"Maaaaan, what the fuck, Joe!" snapped Julie, so pissed that she was literally seeing red.

She'd emptied four clips in less than five minutes. Next to her, Yvette had six empty clips and was working on her fifth. Other officers in their squad were all practicing their shooting. Yvette and Julie were *trying* to relieve some stress by squeezing off a few hundred rounds, visualizing their targets as T.G.'s and Bucks's balls, but it was making them even angrier.

It'd been almost a month since they'd returned back to Illinois. T.G. and Bucks had packed up and all but disappeared. Their phones had been shut off, no addresses for them were listed anywhere. They'd sold every vehicle they had, anything that would put them in a database of any sort had been sold. Yvette and Julie couldn't even find a single one of their dope boys so they could snatch them up and force them to give up their whereabouts.

They tried to focus on work to help them forget about T.G. and Bucks. They'd been in seven shootouts, three high-speed chases, four raids, and had pulled over a passenger coach bus that was carrying not only illegal immigrants that had come from Mexico, but tons of illicit drugs that were found in custom traps built into the bus's undercarriage.

It had been twenty-one very long days, filled with action, but no matter what, all the two could think about was T.G. and Bucks.

Yvette growled as the semi-automatic .357 Taurus she was shooting clicked empty again.

Julie was about to re-load her new Colt CAR-15, when Webster rushed into the shooting range.

"Hey! You two! I need you to roll with me, *right now!*" he stated urgently.

They both looked at him.

"Why? What's goin' on?" Julie asked, with a raised eyebrow.

He looked at them, glanced around at the other officers that were either shooting or reloading, then looked back at them.

"Come out to the parking lot. I'll fill you in out there," he told them.

They followed him out of the range with their guns in their hands, out to the dark parking lot. Walking to where his matte-black Dodge Ram TRX pick-up truck was parked, a nice walk away from where the rear door to the station was, Webster stopped and turned to them.

"I've been watching this guy for the past two years, and I have never been able to catch him doing anything with his own two hands. He's very smart, very resourceful, and really connected. This guy is like the new-age Pablo Escobar, but without blowing up his own people."

Yvette and Julie both felt their hearts thumping in their chests. They had a clue whom their comrade was speaking of, but they prayed they were wrong.

Webster took his iPhone out of his pocket, went into the surveillance photos he had, and showed them. When they saw him, they both cursed under their breaths.

"Benicio Romero, Colombian cocaine king pin from Medellin, but has been living in Illinois for a number of years. He's up there in status with the boss of the *Cartel Jalisco Nueva Generaccion*, and El Chapo. I've just received word from one of my C.I.s that he's actually in one of his own stash houses, a *big* one, right at this moment, waiting for a gigantic shipment to come in."

"Okay…so…what?" asked Julie.

Yvette wondered the same.

"A bust like *this* will make peons like *us* worthy of having superior statuses over hundreds of fellow officers," Webster told them, with a grin. "And *maybe*, it could also earn me a date with the department's most gorgeous officer ever to walk its halls."

Yvette put on the fakest smile ever. Julie almost vomited.

"Persistent," Yvette said, stepping closer to him. "I actually very much admire that in a man, Webster. Maybe if you survive this, we just might be able to go for some Chinese food. I *love* oysters and calamari."

Webster's grin grew even bigger. "Oh, I will survive this, and we will get to enjoy a meal together. Come on. Let's get there and nail this bastard."

***

In Webster's pick-up truck, Yvette and Julie, dressed in full tactical gear, with AR-15s and their utility belts equipped with extra clips and concussion grenades, sat quietly as the Hellcat engine under the hood roared from Webster flooring it north on I-94 towards Antioch, Illinois.

In the backseat, Julie had been texting Benicio non-stop, trying to warn him about the raid that was coming, but he wouldn't reply back. Sighing, she turned her phone off, tucked it into the pocket of her jumpsuit, then she took the Glock 17 she had and checked the clip again.

Up in the front seat, Yvette was deep in thought. She wondered how much Webster had seen or found out. Two years was a *looong* time. She and Julie had been handling business for him for just *over* that amount of time.

T.G. filled the other half of her mind. Thoughts of losing the only man she truly loved to some straight bullshit had her head all fucked up. Her heart was gone now. It no longer existed. Hurt and pain had been her life way too many times. No way was she going to let the only other man that cared for her and Julie be taken down by Webster, especially one that had put millions in their hands.

***

"Okay, ladies. We're approaching our destination," Webster told them, as he got off 94 at Route 173 and headed west to Antioch. "Get ready. This guy is not going to cuff up without a firefight."

He won't have to, bitch, Yvette thought, glad that she'd brought her unregistered Beretta 9mm with her.

"Copy that," Julie said from the back seat.

Riding past the big auto restoration shop, Webster pointed their eyes to it. They all saw the brightly lit front section, filled with ol' schools and new schools. Seeing a path road that was on the side, they all caught a glimpse of a group of guys walking around before their vision was obscured by trees.

At the corner of 173 and Route 45, Webster parked his TRX at a small repair shop next to a gas station. They all got out with their ARs and back-up pistols tucked. Using the cover of night to cross the streets and enter the wooded area next to where Benicio's business was, Yvette and Julie followed behind Webster, closing in on their target's spot.

Reaching the edge of the woods, they all crouched down and looked out from the trees. The rear of the building had six garage door ports. Tall light poles lit the area up brightly, revealing more expensive cars and SUVs.

Standing in a circle was a group of men, all dressed in tactical gear just like them, holding assault rifles just like they were.

"Son of a bitch!" cursed Webster. "He's got cops on payroll, watching the property. This is *waaay* deeper than I thought."

"So, what's the plan?" asked Julie.

Before he could answer, they heard a diesel engine. Looking to their left, they saw a big box truck turn into the front lot of the business. It rolled along the side and entered the back lot. They watched as the driver got lined up with the first garage door port, then back up. The door raised up and the driver backed the truck all the way inside.

The men that were outside stepped in with it, then the garage door closed.

"We are still going in," Webster declared, standing up. "Hope you two didn't drink or eat too much, because it's about to get crazy. Let's go!"

***

They crept fast through the back lot and got to the rear exit door. Yvette and Julie kept their guns up, shifting around and ready to shoot if anyone popped out at them. They got to the door and paused. Webster looked up and around the building's exterior.

"No cameras, that's surprising," he said, as he reached up and gently twisted the doorknob, testing it. "And the door isn't locked. These guys are making this *too* easy. Come on!"

He quietly opened the door, holding it open for them. Once they were inside, he closed and locked it.

They discovered they were in a hallway. At the other end was a door with light coming from the space under it. They crept towards it and heard voices coming from the other side.

Webster turned to Yvette and Julie. He held up a hand and counted down from five. When he reached zero, Webster opened the door and rushed in with his gun up.

Yvette and Julie ran in behind him and were immediately shocked to see Benicio, tied up in a chair, in the middle of the small room. What fucked them up even more, was when they laid eyes on T.G. and Bucks, both tied to chairs right next to Benicio. The three had duct tape over their mouths, preventing them from talking. They had been stripped down to their boxer briefs, and all three of them had bruises all over.

"Webster!" Yvette shouted in shock, looking at a battered T.G. "What the hell is this?"

Julie was stuck with her mouth hanging agape at the sight of Bucks. Her eyes met his and filled with tears.

Webster was still facing away from the ladies, looking at the three men when he spoke.

"You two are the nastiest whores I've ever met, and you two are criminals," he told them, then in the blink of an eye, he lifted up his AR and pointed it at Benicio, pulling the trigger.

-*BOCKA!*-

"Nooo!" the two screamed in unison when Benicio's head exploded. The impact of the shot sent the chair he was in is flying backwards, crashing to the ground. Webster turned the barrel of his gun on T.G. next.

"No! Drop it!" Yvette yelled, pointing *her* AR at the back of Webster's head.

Julie raised her AR at him as well, wrapping her finger around the trigger, gritting her teeth together.

T.G. and Bucks stayed quiet. Neither of them flinched or blinked. They showed no fear at all. Death was an eminent thing. They were in the game, and to the current day, there had never been any successful players.

"Webster! Drop the fucking gun or you die, bitch!" Yvette screamed.

Just then, the sounds of clicking filled the room. Webster started chuckling. Yvette and Julie knew those sounds too well.

They both felt the barrels of guns touch the backs of their own heads. The men in tactical suits came into view from behind them. Two of them took their ARs and their back-up guns, then went and circled around them.

Webster finally turned around and looked at them. He had the most diabolical smirk on his face.

"I told you it was about to get crazy," he said to them. "Now, here's how it's gonna go down."

Two of his crooked partners raised their guns and pointed at T.G. and Bucks.

Yvette and Julie screamed in panic.

"Don't do this! Please, Webster!" Yvette begged, as her heart pounded in her chest. "I'll do anything! Please!"

He laughed. "Oh, *I* am not going to do *anything*, but *you* are," he told her. "Only *one* of these cocksuckers gets to live. Which one will it be, ladies? You have just five seconds to decide, or I will decide, and you won't like my choice," he said.

Yvette and Julie swallowed hard. They looked at the guys and wanted to run to them, shield them with their own bodies.

"Why are you doing this?" Julie pleaded to know. "This isn't right, Webster!"

"That was two seconds out of your time, ladies," Webster spoke again, ignoring her. "If you *don't* choose, I will, then the both of you will die *with* them. What's it gonna be, ladies? *One* of them, or *both* of you?"

To Be Continued…

Lock Down Publications and Ca$h Presents
Assisted Publishing Packages

Due to an increase in the price of services we have increased our prices. The prices below reflect the price increase as of 11/1/24.

BASIC PACKAGE	UPGRADED PACKAGE
$699	$1000
Editing	Typing
Cover Design	Editing
Formatting	Cover Design
	Formatting
	Upload eBooks to Amazon
	Upload Paperback to Amazon
ADVANCE PACKAGE	**LDP SUPREME PACKAGE**
$1,400	$1,700
Typing	Typing
Editing (line editing/content)	Editing (line editing/content)
Cover Design	Cover Design
Formatting	Formatting
Copyright Registration	Copyright Registration
Proofreading	Proofreading
Upload eBooks to Amazon	Set up Amazon Account
Upload Paperback to Amazon	Upload eBooks to Amazon
	Upload Paperback to Amazon
	Advertise on LDP's Amazon and Facebook Page

***Other services available upon request.
Additional charges may apply

Lock Down Publications
P.O. Box 944
Stockbridge, GA 30281-9998
Phone: 470 303-9761
Email: lockdownpublications@gmail.com

Submission Guideline

Submit the first three chapters of your completed manuscript to ldpsubmissions@gmail.com. In the subject line add **Your Book's Title**. The manuscript must be in a Word Doc file and sent as an attachment. Document should be in Times New Roman, double spaced, and in size 12 font. Also, provide your synopsis and full contact information. If sending multiple submissions, they must each be in a separate email.

Have a story but no way to send it electronically? You can still submit to LDP/Ca$h Presents. Send in the first three chapters, written or typed, of your completed manuscript to:

LDP: Submissions Dept
P.O. Box 944
Stockbridge, GA 30281-9998

DO NOT send original manuscript. Must be a duplicate. Provide your synopsis and a cover letter containing your full contact information.

Thanks for considering LDP and Ca$h Presents.

NEW RELEASES

BLOODLINE OF A SAVAGE 1,2&3
THESE VICIOUS STREETS 1,2&3
RELENTLESS GOON
RELENTLESS GOON 2
BY PRINCE A. TAUHID

THE BUTTERFLY MAFIA 1-3
BY FUMIYA PAYNE

A THUG'S STREET PRINCESS 1,2&3
BY MEESHA

CITY OF SMOKE 1& 2
BY MOLOTTI

STEPPERS 1,2&3
THE REAL BADDIES OF CHI-RAQ
BY KING RIO

THE LANE 1&2
BY KEN-KEN SPENCE

THUG OF SPADES 1,2&3
LOVE IN THE TRENCHES 2
CORNER BOY CHRONICLES
BY COREY ROBINSON

TIL DEATH 3
BY ARYANNA

THE BIRTH OF A GANGSTER 4
BY DELMONT PLAYER

CHRISTOPHER "DIESEL" HORNEZES

PRODUCT OF THE STREETS 1&2
BY DEMOND "MONEY" ANDERSON

NO TIME FOR ERROR
BY KEESE

MONEY HUNGRY DEMONS 1,2&3
BY TRANAY ADAMS

HUNGRY FOR MONEY 1&2
BY SLIMBOS

A THUGGISH PASSION
KILLAZ ON STANDBY 1&2
LAND OF DA HOOLIGANZ 1,2&3
FRESH OFF DA PORCH
BY IRA B.

COUNTDOWN OF A KILLA 1&2
GUNS DOWN, BOTTOMS UP 1&2
SEX, MURDA AND GOD
BY LO-LIFE

THE LEVEL UP 1&2
BY LUXURY KING

FO'EVA ROLLIN' 1&2
BY ASSA RAYMOND BAKER

HUB CITY MENACE 1&2
BY J. WHITE

KILLA CREW
DYING FOR LIKES
BY ARYANNA

BAD B*TCHES WIT' GUNZ

IF YOU CROSS ME ONCE 6
ANGEL 5
By Anthony Fields

IMMA DIE BOUT MINE 5
By Aryanna

A THUGS STREET PRINCESS 3
EMBRACING THE LOVE OF A BOSS
By Meesha

PRODUCT OF THE STREETS 3
By Demond Money Anderson

STANDING ON HER BUSINESS
BY DG SANTANA

GET IT IN SLUGS 1&2
B. STALLS

CORNER BOYS 2
By Corey Robinson

THE MURDER QUEENS 6&7
By Michael Gallon

CITY OF SMOKE 3
By Molotti

CONFESSIONS OF A DOPEBOY
By Nicholas Lock

TENDER
BY KHUFU

CHRISTOPHER "DIESEL" HORNEZES

THA TAKEOVER
By Keith Chandler

BETRAYAL OF A G 2
By Ray Vinci

CRIME BOSS 4
By Playa Ray

Coming Soon from Lock Down Publications/Ca$h Presents

RAN OFF ON THE PLUG 2 by **PAPER BOI RARI**
STREET REDEMPTION by **TONY DANIELS**
SAVAGE FAMILY EMPIRE by **PRINCE TAUHID**
BAD BITCHES WIT' GUNZ by **DIESEL**
THE SINGLE LADIES by **DIESEL**
COKE BY THE TRUCKLOAD by **DIESEL**
PROBLEM SOLVED by **DIESEL**
TIPPIN' THE SCALES by **DIESEL**
OPPS CRY TOO by **SAYNOMORE**
A GANGSTA'S KARMA by **FLAME**

CHRISTOPHER "DIESEL" HORNEZES

AVAILABLE NOW

RESTRAINING ORDER 1 & 2
By **CA$H & Coffee**

LOVE KNOWS NO BOUNDARIES 1-3
By **Coffee**

RAISED AS A GOON I, II, III & IV
BRED BY THE SLUMS I, II, III
BLAST FOR ME I & II
ROTTEN TO THE CORE I II III
A BRONX TALE I, II, III
DUFFLE BAG CARTEL I II III IV V VI
HEARTLESS GOON I II III IV V
A SAVAGE DOPEBOY I II
DRUG LORDS I II III
CUTTHROAT MAFIA I II
KING OF THE TRENCHES
By **Ghost**

LAY IT DOWN I & II
LAST OF A DYING BREED I II
BLOOD STAINS OF A SHOTTA I & II III
By **Jamaica**

LOYAL TO THE GAME I II III
LIFE OF SIN I, II III
By **TJ & Jelissa**

IF LOVING HIM IS WRONG...I & II
LOVE ME EVEN WHEN IT HURTS I II III
By **Jelissa**

BAD B*TCHES WIT' GUNZ

PUSH IT TO THE LIMIT
By **Bre' Hayes**

BLOODY COMMAS I & II
SKI MASK CARTEL I, II & III
KING OF NEW YORK I II, III IV V
RISE TO POWER I II III
COKE KINGS I II III IV V
BORN HEARTLESS I II III IV
KING OF THE TRAP I II
By **T.J. Edwards**

WHEN THE STREETS CLAP BACK I & II III
THE HEART OF A SAVAGE I II III IV
MONEY MAFIA I II
LOYAL TO THE SOIL I II III
By **Jibril Williams**

A DISTINGUISHED THUG STOLE MY HEART I - III
LOVE SHOULDN'T HURT I II III IV
RENEGADE BOYS 1-4
PAID IN KARMA 1-3
SAVAGE STORMS 1-3
AN UNFORESEEN LOVE 1-3
BABY, I'M WINTERTIME COLD 1-3
A THUG'S STREET PRINCESS 1&2
By **Meesha**

CUM FOR ME 1-8
An LDP Erotica Collaboration

BLOOD OF A BOSS 1-5
SHADOWS OF THE GAME
TRAP BASTARD
By **Askari**

CHRISTOPHER "DIESEL" HORNEZES

A GANGSTER'S CODE 1-3
A GANGSTER'S SYN 1-3
THE SAVAGE LIFE 1-3
CHAINED TO THE STREETS 1-3
BLOOD ON THE MONEY 1-3
A GANGSTA'S PAIN 1-3
BEAUTIFUL LIES AND UGLY TRUTHS
CHURCH IN THESE STREETS
By **J-Blunt**

THE STREETS BLEED MURDER 1-3
THE HEART OF A GANGSTA 1-3
By **Jerry Jackson**

WHEN A GOOD GIRL GOES BAD
By **Adrienne**

THE COST OF LOYALTY 1-3
By **Kweli**

BRIDE OF A HUSTLA 1-3
THE FETTI GIRLS 1-3
CORRUPTED BY A GANGSTA 1-4
BLINDED BY HIS LOVE
THE PRICE YOU PAY FOR LOVE 1-3
DOPE GIRL MAGIC 1-3
By **Destiny Skai**

A KINGPIN'S AMBITION
A KINGPIN'S AMBITION II
I MURDER FOR THE DOUGH
By **Ambitious**

A DOPEBOY'S PRAYER
By **Eddie "Wolf" Lee**

BAD B*TCHES WIT' GUNZ

TRUE SAVAGE 1-7
DOPE BOY MAGIC 1-3
MIDNIGHT CARTEL 1-3
CITY OF KINGZ 1&2
NIGHTMARE ON SILENT AVE
THE PLUG OF LIL MEXICO 1&2
CLASSIC CITY
By **Chris Green**

LOVE & CHASIN' PAPER
By **Qay Crockett**

THE KING CARTEL 1-3
By **Frank Gresham**

THESE NIGGAS AIN'T LOYAL 1-3
By **Nikki Tee**

GANGSTA SHYT 1-3
By **CATO**

THE ULTIMATE BETRAYAL
By **Phoenix**

BOSS'N UP 1-3
By **Royal Nicole**

I LOVE YOU TO DEATH
By **Destiny J**

BROOKLYN HUSTLAZ
By **Boogsy Morina**

GANGSTA CITY
By **Teddy Duke**

CHRISTOPHER "DIESEL" HORNEZES

TO DIE IN VAIN
SINS OF A HUSTLA
By **ASAD**

I RIDE FOR MY HITTA
I STILL RIDE FOR MY HITTA
By **Misty Holt**

A GANGSTER'S REVENGE 1-4
THE BOSS MAN'S DAUGHTERS 1-5
A SAVAGE LOVE 1&2
BAE BELONGS TO ME 1&2
A HUSTLER'S DECEIT 1-3
WHAT BAD BITCHES DO 1-3
SOUL OF A MONSTER 1-3
KILL ZONE
A DOPE BOY'S QUEEN 1-3
TIL DEATH 1-3
IMMA DIE BOUT MINE 1-5
By **Aryanna**

BROOKLYN ON LOCK 1 & 2
By **Sonovia**

A DRUG KING AND HIS DIAMOND 1-3
A DOPEMAN'S RICHES
HER MAN, MINE'S TOO 1&2
CASH MONEY HO'S
THE WIFEY I USED TO BE 1&2
PRETTY GIRLS DO NASTY THINGS
By **Nicole Goosby**

THE STREETS ARE CALLING
By **Duquie Wilson**

BAD B*TCHES WIT' GUNZ

LIPSTICK KILLAH 1-3
CRIME OF PASSION 1-3
FRIEND OR FOE 1-3
By **Mimi**

TRAPHOUSE KING 1-3
KINGPIN KILLAZ 1-3
STREET KINGS 1&2
PAID IN BLOOD 1&2
CARTEL KILLAZ 1-3
DOPE GODS 1&2
By **Hood Rich**

STEADY MOBBN' 1-3
THE STREETS STAINED MY SOUL 1-3
By **Marcellus Allen**

WHO SHOT YA 1-3
SON OF A DOPE FIEND 1-4
HEAVEN GOT A GHETTO 1&2
SKI MASK MONEY 1&2
By **Renta**

GORILLAZ IN THE BAY 1-4
TEARS OF A GANGSTA 1/&2
3X KRAZY 1&2
STRAIGHT BEAST MODE 1&2
By **DE'KARI**

TRIGGADALE 1-3
MURDA WAS THE CASE 1-3
By **Elijah R. Freeman**

MARRIED TO A BOSS 1-3
By **Destiny Skai & Chris Green**

CHRISTOPHER "DIESEL" HORNEZES

SLAUGHTER GANG 1-3
RUTHLESS HEART 1-3
By **Willie Slaughter**

GOD BLESS THE TRAPPERS 1-3
THESE SCANDALOUS STREETS 1-3
FEAR MY GANGSTA 1-5
THESE STREETS DON'T LOVE NOBODY 1-2
BURY ME A G 1-5
A GANGSTA'S EMPIRE 1-4
THE DOPEMAN'S BODYGAURD 1&2
THE REALEST KILLAZ 1-3
THE LAST OF THE OGS 1-3
By **Tranay Adams**

KINGZ OF THE GAME 1-7
CRIME BOSS 1-4
By **Playa Ray**

FUK SHYT
By **Blakk Diamond**

DON'T F#CK WITH MY HEART 1&2
By **Linnea**

ADDICTED TO THE DRAMA 1-3
IN THE ARM OF HIS BOSS
By **Jamila**

LOYALTY AIN'T PROMISED 1&2
By **Keith Williams**

FOREVER GANGSTA 1&2
GLOCKS ON SATIN SHEETS 1&2
By **Adrian Dulan**

BAD B*TCHES WIT' GUNZ

YAYO 1-4
A SHOOTER'S AMBITION 1&2
BRED IN THE GAME
By **S. Allen**

TRAP GOD 1-3
RICH $AVAGE 1-3
MONEY IN THE GRAVE 1-3
CARTEL MONEY
By **Martell Troublesome Bolden**

TOE TAGZ 1-4
LEVELS TO THIS SHYT 1&2
IT'S JUST ME AND YOU
By **Ah'Million**

KINGPIN DREAMS 1-3
RAN OFF ON DA PLUG
By **Paper Boi Rari**

THE STREETS MADE ME 1-3
By **Larry D. Wright**

CONFESSIONS OF A GANGSTA 1-4
CONFESSIONS OF A JACKBOY 1-3
CONFESSIONS OF A HITMAN
By **Nicholas Lock**

I'M NOTHING WITHOUT HIS LOVE
SINS OF A THUG
TO THE THUG I LOVED BEFORE
A GANGSTA SAVED XMAS
IN A HUSTLER I TRUST
By **Monet Dragun**

CHRISTOPHER "DIESEL" HORNEZES

QUIET MONEY 1-3
THUG LIFE 1-3
EXTENDED CLIP 1&2
A GANGSTA'S PARADISE
By **Trai'Quan**

CAUGHT UP IN THE LIFE 1-3
THE STREETS NEVER LET GO 1-3
By **Robert Baptiste**

NEW TO THE GAME 1-3
MONEY, MURDER & MEMORIES 1-3
By **Malik D. Rice**

THE LIFE OF A HOOD STAR
By **Ca$h & Rashia Wilson**

THE STREETS WILL NEVER CLOSE 1-4
By **K'ajji**

LIFE OF A SAVAGE 1-4
A GANGSTA'S QUR'AN 1-4
MURDA SEASON 1-3
GANGLAND CARTEL 1-3
CHI'RAQ GANGSTAS 1-4
KILLERS ON ELM STREET 1-3
JACK BOYZ N DA BRONX 1-3
A DOPEBOY'S DREAM 1-3
JACK BOYS VS DOPE BOYS 1-3
COKE GIRLZ
COKE BOYS
SOSA GANG 1&2
BRONX SAVAGES
BODYMORE KINGPINS
BLOOD OF A GOON
By **Romell Tukes**

BAD B*TCHES WIT' GUNZ

CREAM 2-3
THE STREETS WILL TALK
By **Yolanda Moore**

CONCRETE KILLA 1-3
VICIOUS LOYALTY 1-3
By **Kingpen**

THE ULTIMATE SACRIFICE 1-6
KHADIFI
IF YOU CROSS ME ONCE 1-5
ANGEL 1-4
IN THE BLINK OF AN EYE
By **Anthony Fields**

NIGHTMARES OF A HUSTLA 1-3
BLOOD AND GAMES 1&2
By **King Dream**

HARD AND RUTHLESS 1&2
MOB TOWN 251
THE BILLIONAIRE BENTLEYS 1-3
REAL G'S MOVE IN SILENCE
By **Von Diesel**

MOB TIES 1-7
SOUL OF A HUSTLER, HEART OF A KILLER 1-3
GORILLAZ IN THE TRENCHES
By **SayNoMore**

BODYMORE MURDERLAND 1-3
THE BIRTH OF A GANGSTER 1-4
By **Delmont Player**

FOR THE LOVE OF A BOSS 1&2
By **C. D. Blue**

CHRISTOPHER "DIESEL" HORNEZES

KILLA KOUNTY 1-5
By **Khufu**

MOBBED UP 1-4
THE BRICK MAN 1-5
THE COCAINE PRINCESS 1-10
STEPPERS 1-3
SUPER GREMLIN 1-4
By **King Rio**

MONEY GAME 1&2
By **Smoove Dolla**

A GANGSTA'S KARMA 1-4
By **FLAME**

KING OF THE TRENCHES 1-3
By **GHOST & TRANAY ADAMS**

QUEEN OF THE ZOO 1&2
By **Black Migo**

GRIMEY WAYS 1-3
BETRAYAL OF A G
By **Ray Vinci**

XMAS WITH AN ATL SHOOTER
By **Ca$h & Destiny Skai**

KING KILLA 1&2
By **Vincent "Vitto" Holloway**

BETRAYAL OF A THUG 1&2
By **Fre$h**

BAD B*TCHES WIT' GUNZ

THE MURDER QUEENS 1-6
By **Michael Gallon**

FOR THE LOVE OF BLOOD 1-4
By **Jamel Mitchell**

HOOD CONSIGLIERE 1&2
NO TIME FOR ERROR
By **Keese**

PROTÉGÉ OF A LEGEND 1&2
LOVE IN THE TRENCHES 1&2
By **Corey Robinson**

THE PLUG'S RUTHLESS DAUGHTER 1&2
By **Tony Daniels**

BORN IN THE GRAVE 1-3
CRIME PAYS 1&2
By **Self Made Tay**

MOAN IN MY MOUTH
By **XTASY**

TORN BETWEEN A GANGSTER AND A
GENTLEMAN
By **J-BLUNT & Miss Kim**

HERE TODAY GONE TOMORROW 1&2
By **Fly Rock**

PILLOW PRINCESS
By **S. Hawkins**

SANCTIFIED AND HORNY
by **XTASY**

CHRISTOPHER "DIESEL" HORNEZES

WOMEN LIE MEN LIE 1-4
FIFTY SHADES OF SNOW 1-3
STACK BEFORE YOU SPLURGE
GIRLS FALL LIKE DOMINOES
NAÏVE TO THE STREETS
By **ROY MILLIGAN**

LOYALTY IS EVERYTHING 1-3
CITY OF SMOKE 1&2
By **Molotti**

THE BUTTERFLY MAFIA 1-4
SALUTE MY SAVAGERY 1&2
By **Fumiya Payne**

THE LANE 1&2
By **Ken-Ken Spence**

THE PUSSY TRAP 1-5
By **Nene Capri**

DIRTY DNA
By **Blaque**

BOOKS BY LDP'S CEO, CA$H

TRUST IN NO MAN
TRUST IN NO MAN 2
TRUST IN NO MAN 3
BONDED BY BLOOD
SHORTY GOT A THUG
THUGS CRY
THUGS CRY 2
THUGS CRY 3
TRUST NO BITCH
TRUST NO BITCH 2
TRUST NO BITCH 3
TIL MY CASKET DROPS
RESTRAINING ORDER
RESTRAINING ORDER 2
IN LOVE WITH A CONVICT
LIFE OF A HOOD STAR
XMAS WITH AN ATL SHOOTER

www.ingramcontent.com/pod-product-compliance
Lightning Source LLC
Chambersburg PA
CBHW071231260626
47162CB00004B/1516